CW01642169

AGENT RED

By

Mark Reddan

ISBN 978-1-7399600-0-1

This book is intended for readers 18+ and contains material that may be disturbing to some, such as graphic violence and explicit scenes.

All characters in this book are fictitious, and any resemblance to actual persons, living or dead, is purely coincidental.

This book is dedicated to my wife, Sarah.

Without whose support, none of this would have been possible.

Foreword

Thank you for reading this book. It is one of my proudest moments and the result of a lot of hours and hard work.

I'd love to connect with you and hear your feedback;

Facebook as Mark Reddan Author

Email: markreddanauthor@gmail.com

www.markreddan.co.uk

Part One

1

The car turned slowly into the street. Its engine reverberated against the houses and echoed, amplifying the sound. It pulled up outside the house, its engine died. The man inside just sat there looking at the place he had arrived at cautiously, taking in everything he could about it from his viewpoint.
It looked like a traditional stereotypical terraced house, nothing special. It was painted cream with white window dressing, and it required attention and repainting. Small steps were leading up to the front door with a small plant on each side, trying to make the entrance seem more upmarket than it was. The plants were dying. They failed.
Logan Taylor picked up the tablet from the seat, opened it, waited for the little indication that it was secure, and opened up the information. It was a waste of time as he had read, re-read, and re-read all the information again and again, but it was always better to be over-prepared, and it gave him cover if anyone walked past.
It showed a picture of a man, probably his driving license photo judging from the image. Next to it was his name, BRANDON HOUTON, along with all his details. He was 5'11 with scruffy, dirty blonde hair, pale blue eyes that looked almost opaque and his skin tone looked pale yellow, but the skin and eye tone may be the quality of the picture. It showed what he liked to eat, where he liked to shop, his job, his friends, his girlfriends (yes, more than one, it seemed Brandon had difficulty staying faithful) and his address...this

address, the house in need of attention and repair that had dying plants at the front door.
Taylor had a good view of the street from his position, and once he was sure no one was around to see him, he placed the file under the passenger seat, so it was hidden from view and after taking one last glance around to make sure, he exited the car.
It was a bleak day, overcast, but it looked like the rain may hold off. The clouds blocked the sun, and it cast an almost grey filter across the world. Everything looked bleak, washed out, as if the weather had given up on the day and was just riding it out, waiting for tomorrow to see if it was going to get any better.

Taylor stretched himself out and started to walk to the end of the street slowly, pretended to tie his shoe and scooped up the tiny camera from the neighbour's plant pot he had placed to watch the front of the house. He was wearing a black 3-piece suit, a white shirt with a deep red tie and black gloves. He was about 5'10 with dark brown hair that had started to grey, brown eyes and wore black Converse hi-top shoes. The suit was bespoke and fit him perfectly. Taylor had always made a point of wearing clothes that fit correctly, it was a pride thing he had, and it meant he could move without the hindrance of too tight or too loose clothing. Important.
He reached the end of the road, took a right and walked around and up an access road that ran between the rows of houses. It was used for the rubbish collection and emergency services, so it was quiet; bin day wasn't for a few days yet, so nobody was putting out any last-minute waste.

He found the back gate that led to Brandon's house. It was old and not well secured; Brandon had been cautious about securing the front of his house but hadn't been bothered to give the same attention to the rear. It was a small blue gate with a wall on either side. The walls were deteriorating and had chunks missing from years of being weather-worn and not repaired. Once he retrieved the other camera hidden on the wall opposite the gate, it was easy to scale the wall, and Taylor dispatched it in seconds. This put him in the backyard; it was more of a courtyard with decking and a couple of garden chairs with a little side table. They looked as if they were a set. Taylor moved cautiously to the back door. Once there, he took out his lock picks and after a few seconds, he heard the satisfying click that meant he had beat the tumblers and was awarded access. Taylor put the picks away and slowly turned the handle. As he pushed, he looked for any security devices that he may be able to see that would be tripped if the door opened. He couldn't see any. He cautiously pushed the door, and once he was happy nothing was waiting for him, he withdrew his Glock 34 handgun from its holster under his left arm pit, took the silencer from his jacket pocket and secured it, checked the magazine, released the safety and with as much noise as a shadow he moved into the house.
He found himself in the kitchen. He knew that because he knew the layout, the only thing he wasn't sure about was where in the house Brandon would be. Brandon had been a busy boy recently, with many late nights and meetings in dark car parks; so, logic dictated that he should be in bed given his large amount of nocturnal activities. That wasn't a given, however, and just

because Taylor hadn't seen him moving about doesn't mean he wasn't.
Caution was key.
Taylor cleared the kitchen fast. It wasn't difficult. It was basically a square at the back of the house. Nowhere to hide if he knew someone was coming. It had all the appliances you would expect and a small dining table with two chairs, one at each end, in the corner. There was a pile of dirty dishes in the sink and more on the side. There was a calendar on the side of the fridge, one with women in different poses, much like ones found in mechanics garages. Not tasteful. But nothing was written on it, and it was two months behind.
Taylor slowly made his way through into the living room. He peered around the corner first and held his weapon close to his chest, ready to use if required; it always bothered him how on TV shows and films, they always walk around with their weapons far out in front...if anyone were hiding around any corner, they could quickly disarm them before they even saw the threat. Or how they hold their weapon out straight, so as soon as they discharged, they would snap their elbow on the recoil. No. Taylor held his weapon in a tight, two-handed grip, nozzle facing slightly down, against his chest. It allowed him infinitely more manoeuvrability when doing things like this and meant that he wasn't compromised moving through a confined space and got caught off guard.
The living room was simple. It had a cream carpet, white walls, a small leather sofa with a coffee table in front, and judging from the dirt on and around it; the coffee table was used to put his feet up. There was also a small damp patch on the carpet under it; Houton must

have spilt something and moved the table to hide it. There was a TV on the wall opposite the sofa and a net curtain across the window. Taylor could see the front of his Jaguar parked outside the next house up. After a scan of the room, there wasn't anywhere for Brandon to hide in here either, so he moved slowly (the carpet helping mask his footsteps) into the hallway. He was standing opposite a staircase that curved around and out of sight. To his left, down the hall, was the front door. There was no porch, so the front access was visible. There was a door to the cupboard under the stairs, and Taylor moved carefully down, still ready, still alert, slowing when he reached the door. He reached for the handle and carefully turned it. He knew Brandon was dangerous and clever, and he wasn't prepared to assume that the house wasn't protected in case someone came after him.

Someone like Taylor.

He opened the door a crack, looking for any trip wires or danger; it was clear. Taylor opened the door fully to find a shoe closet with coats hanging on hooks. There was no order or neatness to this cupboard. Shoes, loose bags, and items were laid haphazardly on the floor. Brandon was not a man of cleanliness.

Taylor made his way back toward the stairs. There was a clock in the hallway, and the constant rhythmic ticking was almost deafening in the otherwise silent house. He couldn't even hear any sounds from outside, no people, no passing cars, no cats purring, or birds chirping.

Quiet.

Too quiet.

Allowing himself a half-smile at his thought, he made his way up the stairs. He hated stairs; they creaked and sagged and were always at risk of giving away that you were coming. But Brandon wasn't downstairs, so he must be upstairs. Taylor had learnt that the best way to approach stairs was slowly, carefully, and always, whenever possible, stick to the outer edges. People walked up and down stairs all the time, and they did it in the middle, habit, he supposed, and because, well, why wouldn't you? But this is what made stairs wear and creak and sag. He took every step because trying to push up two at a time when trying to be quiet was silly, as it put you off balance. This could make you misstep, and if whoever you were coming after realised it and came to the top of the stairs to repel you, you didn't want to be off-balance. Not having the high ground was bad enough; you need to keep as much as you can on your side.

Taylor reached the top of the stairs without anyone being there to repel him and checked the corners.

Clear.

He was standing facing a door across the landing to a bedroom. Bedroom 2 - he had designated it when planning – to his right, there was a small landing with a bathroom backed onto the stairs and on the other side of the landing next to bedroom 2 was, appropriately, bedroom 1.

Taylor took the step across, moving to the closed door of bedroom 2. He knew one of these rooms held Brandon, but which one?

He leaned close to the door, strained to listen, and held his breath. No sound. Again, with painful slowness, he turned the handle, once again, checking for any form of device or alarm, then he slowly pushed it open. The door creaked; the world stopped. Taylor held his breath, ready to combat anyone who came at him.

After a moment that felt like an hour, nothing had happened, so he slowly made his way into the room, checking the corners for surprises as he did so. Nothing.

Bedroom 2 was actually what looked like a basic - very basic - office. There was a computer table with a laptop plugged in, it wasn't his reason for being here, but part of his assignment was to retrieve data. He made a mental note to come back and get it once he had dealt with Brandon. Once the room had been cleared, easy enough as there was no furniture other than the table and laptop, no wardrobe or built-in storage for him to search, he made his way to the bathroom, it was next door, so it made sense. Once again, he repeated his entry method, and once again, finding no apparent traps, he entered.

The bathroom was small, and ironically, didn't have a bath – just a shower unit with a bottle of shower gel covered in grime on the bottom. A toilet on the back wall and a bathroom cabinet occupied the wall space above the sink. Mould was apparent, visible on the walls, and the smell was the overpowering aroma of damp. Taylor was grateful the room was small, and given no man could hide in the cabinet, he retreated back to the hallway after a quick scan. As a rule, once a door was open, Taylor would not close it again. There is no point risking more creaking doors or the knock of a door closing again to warn people you are there.

That left one. One door. The last door. This was it. Taylor steeled his resolve. It was different when he was clearing a place; there was always a chance of surprise, a gamble almost, of which room will contain his quarry, but at times like this, when there was only one option, he knew the rules were different. He knew in that room. In bedroom 1 was Brandon Houton. Fact. As a famous detective had once said:

'When you have eliminated the impossible, whatever remains, however improbable, must be the truth.'

Taylor had eliminated the rest of the house. What remained was this final room; therefore, Brandon Houton was in that room.
This was exciting for Taylor. He could feel it, the excitement coursing through him, his nerves becoming sharp, his muscles twitched in readiness to respond and react to what was coming. He approached the door, listened. Nothing. Silence. He must be asleep; he has no idea what comes next…
Or does he?
Is he asleep?
Is he waiting behind that door?
Taylor knew sooner or later he would die. Everybody did. But he doubted it would be old age that would be his cause of death. Would Brandon Houton be it? Would this be the last door he would breach? The last house he would search?
Maybe.
Maybe not.
He had a choice to make now. Feather approach or hammer? Soft or loud? There was every chance Houton didn't know Taylor was in the house, and the bang could give him away. Or he could be waiting, with a gun aimed at the door, and as soon as it starts to move, he could empty it through the door, and that would be game over. Had he heard the creaking of the other doors?

All these thoughts went through Taylor's head in less than a second as he calculated what his approach would be.
The feather approach had worked so far, so he decided he would use it. His hand grasped the door handle, slowly turning it, the faint click, as the door released from its latch. Nothing, just the clock ticking from the hallway.
And a hissing.
What was that?
Taylor pushed into the room, with his weapon ready, poised to react. He went in faster than planned, but the hissing noise had set off alarm bells to him. Something was wrong. Taylor aimed his Glock at every inch of the room, but it was left wanting. The space was empty. Just a single bed with a wardrobe, and that was it. Taylor moved his way to the wardrobe and gave it a second, allowing the occupant a moment to panic, and lash out, to burst out from his hiding place, and try and use the element of surprise to overpower him. It wouldn't work, but he let them try anyway.
Nothing happened. No one came bursting out of the wardrobe at him. No one tried to take him by surprise. Taylor opened the doors to the wardrobe fast, bracing to shoot or fight. Nothing. Empty other than clothes and boxes on a shelf.
He holstered his gun. Something wasn't right. Where was he? The house was clear. The cameras he had planted had seen him enter the house, so where was he? It took a moment for recognition to sink in... The hissing! It hadn't been coming from inside the room; it had been coming from the other bedroom…
The laptop!

Taylor bolted out the room, and then he saw it, in the corner, high up on the wall. The camera.
"Shit", he breathed.
Brandon knew he was there. Somehow, he had got back out of the house and was watching him. He moved to bedroom 2 to find the laptop smoking. It looked like the hard drive had been destroyed. Maybe a virus or something Brandon had activated once he had been detected. Taylor didn't know; he wasn't a computer guy. He unplugged it and took it anyway. He quickly searched for anything else that would deem valuable but came up short. He made his way down the stairs and was about to make his way out through the back again when he heard something, something faint, it set his internal alarm off, and he paused. He placed the laptop on the floor just inside the living room. He was sure it was coming from below,
But it was a two-storey house. He reasoned.
A spark lit itself in his stomach; maybe not, maybe he had been so focused that he forgot to look at all the options. Taylor opened the cupboard under the stairs again. The shoes and the mess, something wasn't right, the way they were laid out maybe…
Maybe.
A noise again. Still faint, but louder this time. A false wall? A false wall, he had missed a false wall! It wasn't a door for a cupboard under the stairs. It was a basement that Houton had made to look like one. How had he missed that?
Foolish!
Taylor ran his fingers along the seams and applied a bit of weight, and it moved, then it opened.

'Whatever remains, however improbable, must be the truth.'

Stone steps were leading to an old basement space. Taylor drew his gun and slowly moved down. He was down here; he had to be. Houton hadn't left, and he wasn't in any of the other rooms. He must have seen him on the video, panicked and wiped the laptop. He reached the bottom of the stairs to find what he had been looking for. There were wall charts like ones seen in films of buildings, plans and blueprints, another laptop, and an electronic tablet. But no Brandon.

Damn.

No, he's here.

It was dark, and there were plenty of places to hide down here and not be seen instantly. Taylor kept his guard up. Every hair was on end, and he knew what was coming. He knew it, but would he see it in time? Would he be able to react to it? If Brandon shot him now, he wouldn't even know it had happened. Did he have a gun?

The answer came almost as he thought the question. Taylor saw a flash of metal in motion out of the corner of his eye, a pipe, maybe? Or a golf club? It didn't matter. He tried to move so the hit would roll off him, but it hit him nonetheless, it cracked his shoulder, and Taylor cried out in pain.

The gun fell to the floor, and Taylor turned to meet his attacker. He swung again - as people holding things often do. They think it gives them power, but once you know about it, it can be a hindrance - as Houton swung his arms back to get momentum Taylor moved in close, grabbed the golf club with his left hand and using the momentum he had gained on the move he slammed his right fist into Brandon's ribs. Now it was Brandon's turn to cry out as he let go of the club. He brought his elbow down onto Taylor's back, right between the shoulder blades, and Taylor dropped to one knee and brought the club down with his left hand to Brandon's knee cap. The grip was weak as he wasn't holding it properly, but it was enough to cause some pain and make Brandon retreat a pace so he could get his composure.

Taylor took his chance and lunged at Brandon, who was able to block Taylor's right punch and the left and countered with his own right. Taylor grabbed his wrist with his left hand, moving into his body and flipped him over his thigh. Brandon hit the floor but didn't stay down. He instantly rolled, swung his leg, and took Taylor's out from underneath him. Taylor hit the floor, realised his gun was close and reached for it, hoping to grab it before Brandon was on top of him. His fingers stroked the grip, and he turned to see why Brandon hadn't got on top of him, raining punches, but through the darkness, he saw him making his way to the stairs. He was running for it.

Taylor rolled and, in one motion, scooped up his weapon and was on his feet, giving chase. He saw Brandon move to the living room, and he reached the door to a realisation…

Where had the laptop he had left on the floor gone?

Taylor saw it just in time, and he ducked and rolled, the laptop hitting the wall. Brandon dropped it and hurled himself at Taylor.

Taylor was faster, though and brought a knee up to meet him. It hit him in the jaw and sent him flying. He raised his gun, but Brandon was quick and moved, then he was up and coming again. In the cold hard light of day, Taylor could see Brandon clearly. He was wearing a t-shirt that had probably started its life as white but was now a dirty, yellow-brown and combat trousers that rustled when he moved. His features were the same as the image Taylor had been supplied - not the image quality then - as his skin was more yellow up close, and his eyes were so pale you could almost see through them.

He came in with his shoulder, taking Taylor off balance and then he punched his ribs. Taylor blocked one to his jaw, but the punches just kept coming. The page in the file about his combat training flashed in his mind. This is why Taylor had wanted to be quiet; he knew Brandon could fight.

Taylor had his arms raised to protect his face as the onslaught just kept coming. He had to end this. He sidestepped and brushed off the latest punch, absorbing it into his shoulder. He feinted a punch and kicked him as hard as he could in the knee. Brandon dropped, and Taylor brought his up and hit him in the jaw. His head shot back, and he hit the floor.

Taylor grabbed his gun from the floor, but he was kicked hard in the chest as he turned. He left the ground and ended up on his back on the sofa. He scrambled for purchase, kicking Brandon as he tried to jump on him. Taylor clambered off the sofa, now there was the coffee table between them, and as Brandon turned to run, Taylor grabbed the edge of the table and flipped it at him, it caught his legs, and he fell. It was then he saw it.

A bomb.

Brandon had rigged a bomb under the table. The stain on the carpet wasn't from a drink; it was from when he

placed a goddamn bomb under his goddamn coffee table!
It must be a contingency, a backup.
It had been dormant, but as the table crashed into Brandon, a red light had appeared, and it began ticking, not like the clock in the hallway, but a faster, almost countdown ticking. Brandon was scrambling to get up. He knew what was coming, and so did Taylor. The weighing up of his options took a nano-second before he grabbed his gun and jumped for the window. Brandon hadn't even gathered himself up when it detonated.
The sound was deafening. It wasn't a massive explosion, and it seemed it was only designed to take out the house with minimal damage to the neighbouring homes, but it was enough.
The noise. The heat. The energy.
It propelled Taylor through the window. Thankfully, he had curled himself up as much as he could into a ball as the sheer force ejected him from the room. Glass shattered, and he could feel it scratch his face, his hands, shredding through his clothes, like a thousand tiny needles stabbing him. He hit the pavement and rolled, stopping when he collided with the car parked outside.
Taylor's world had been rocked. He couldn't hear anything other than a ringing in his ears, and he couldn't focus his vision on anything. Everything was blurry. His head pounded; he felt blood dripping from his body as every inch of him stung and ached. Black smoke was billowing out from what remained of the house, and Taylor had ingested a large amount of it. His nose felt clogged, and he coughed, trying to clear

his airways and suck fresh air in. His lungs burned as if they were on fire.

Taylor coughed and spluttered, trying to get up, but his body failed him. He tried to sit up, but again his body failed him. His hands felt numb, and his brain felt like it had been through a blender. He could hear his heartbeat like a drum in his ears. Slowly, things came back to him. He could feel his fingers and his limbs, and while they hurt like hell, he was able to right himself. He used the car, a silver Vauxhall Astra, which no longer had any windows, it seemed, as he cut his hand gripping the door frame, to help him get up all the way. It was a disaster. It looked like, well, like a bomb had gone off. The neighbouring houses were still standing, although all the windows had been relinquished of their glass. Brandon Houton's house hadn't completely gone. Structurally it still stood. It just didn't have a front at all anymore. It looked like the kitchen wasn't in great shape either. The fridge had fallen over, and the dirty dishes had been blown out of the sink, smashed, and were littering the floor.
Taylor wondered if anything had survived. He coughed and unsteady, holding his ribs, he climbed his way back through the rubble into the house. He could see parts of Brandon's body lying around that had been entirely destroyed by the detonation, they were charred, and the skin was severely burned and almost peeling off. Taylor could smell the repulsive aroma of burnt flesh even through the thick smoke that filled his nose. Small fires were burning, and, for a moment, he felt sorry for him. That cannot have been a nice way to go. Taylor climbed down the stairs to the basement, but it seemed that whatever Brandon had done to the

laptop in the bedroom, he had replicated here. Most of the tech had survived the blast, with only the paperwork on the wall burning from the fire, but it was all useless.
This was not how it was supposed to go. Taylor cursed himself as he made his way back to the street, unsure on his feet and nearly stumbling as he climbed down the rubble. Taylor brushed himself off. Amazingly the road wasn't crowded with people, all looking, but maybe they were still at work or something. Either way, it wouldn't be long – time to leave.
He glanced down to make sure he was ok and all still in one piece. His suit was ruined, which was annoying, but he still had all his limbs attached, so that was something.
Taylor gingerly made his way to the Jaguar. He groaned as he climbed in and sank into the leather seat, starting the engine. Usually, he loved to hear his car start up, the deep growl of the V8, but right now, all he could hear was the ringing. It was definitely not safe to drive, but he had to get some distance between him and this scene.
His head was still pounding, and he couldn't focus straight. Nonetheless, he put the car in gear, pulled out and tore down the street.

He decided that jumping through a window as a building explodes is way less fun than it looks on TV.

2

Craftsman Bespoke Tattooing was an unassuming building, in the middle of an average row of shops, in the middle of an average UK street. It was a white, three-storey building with grey panelling along the bottom of the windows. The sign was black-backed with gold *'Craftsman'* lettering and white *'Bespoke Tattooing'* underneath. It was a simple layout but looked clean and classy. An old pub-style sign hung from the wall on the left side of the building with the Craftsman logo and a flourishing mandala design around it swinging gently in the soft breeze. The windows were framed in white, and the main glass front of the shop was frosted over completely with just the Craftsman logo matching the swing sign and 'Private Studio' underneath in the middle. There was limited space available out the front for parking to accommodate all the shops and businesses, but thankfully today, a space was vacant right outside. Taylor did not want to walk from the car park around the corner or around the row of buildings to get to the back entrance. It was only a couple of minutes' walk, and usually, he preferred the car park as it kept the Jaguar out of view as its metallic red paint stood out like a sore thumb against the usual black, grey and silver of the sedans, SUVs and hatchbacks. However, today he was thankful for the short walk. He had managed to regain some of his cognitive functions and had managed to drive without crashing, which was a blessing, and once the ringing in his ears had reduced enough, he had been able to use his phone and call the office. Taylor had explained what had happened and that the primary assignment was completed. However, the secondary had failed due to complications. The response had been simply:

Report back for debrief.

So here he was.
He eased himself out of the Jaguar and cursed himself for not taking one of the bigger cars, a low two-seater sports car such as his F-Type SVR wasn't the easiest to get out when you felt like your ribs had been crushed, and you had just gone ten rounds with a professional boxer. Oh, and the whole being blown clear out of a building by a bomb strapped under a coffee table. That didn't help.
Maybe he should go back to using Company cars.
Once he was (ungracefully) out, he straightened up as best he could. His ribs were still in agony. He winced and moved his hand to them to try and ease some of the pain. It didn't help. His head still throbbed and felt like a train had hit him. Every noise seemed amplified; just the people walking past felt like a jackhammer to his ears and his lungs still burned as he coughed up again.
He made the short journey to the tattoo studio and pushed the door. A tiny bell above the door rang to announce a guest, and two tattoo artists looked up to see who had entered their house of work.
While the outside of the tattoo studio had been classy yet conservative, much more subtle than most studios in the city, inside was like another world. As Taylor entered, he was treated with a small mat to wipe his feet. Next to him was an umbrella holder; it was empty as it hadn't rained for a few days. The smell of ink hit

his nostrils; it was a comforting smell and completely defeated the air freshener that was trying to make the room smell like a summer meadow or wild berries or something to that effect. Next to it was a small fridge that housed cans of fizzy drinks for clients if their sugar level got low during a tattoo session or just if they wanted one. In front of him were two Chesterfield sofas facing each other with a glass-topped coffee table in the middle and a couple of books - the artists' portfolios - sitting proudly on top. If Taylor never saw another coffee table again, it would be too soon. At least this one was glass-topped, so he could see nothing sinister was lurking underneath it. The floor was all wood effect, easy to clean, spreading to the back of the building where the artists were busy working. The walls were split into two sections. The lower half was wood cladding, a deep wood that looked like it belonged in an old English gentleman's house. The top half was painted a crisp, clean white, decorated with tattoo designs in clean black, simple frames. It felt refreshing just to look at it. The furniture, tattoo station equipment and decorations were all glossy black and contrasted with the white beautifully. A small gap and a couple of steps raised the level between the waiting area and the tattoo stations. The two areas looked perfect together, but just that small change made it clear that one was waiting and one was where the work happened.

Having glanced up at the intrusion, the artists soon put their heads back down and continued working on their clients. One of which Taylor recognised, a man was getting something dark, mean, and moody on his chest. The other client, a woman he didn't recognise, looked to be getting some coloured floral work done on her.

Both the clients were on opposite sides of the room, their backs to him and there were dividers available for privacy, but neither had opted to use them. The studio was narrow but long, and there was still plenty of room between them.
The artists were dressed identically. They both wore black trousers, a black shirt with a black waistcoat and a white tie. They were not bespoke made; they were off the peg, out of a shop items. They were wearing black disposable aprons, disposable sleeve protectors over their shirt sleeves and black gloves. One had a neck tattoo visible above the collar line, but the other didn't. From his appearance, he looked to be without any tattoos, but Taylor knew better.
Taylor himself had many tattoos, but in his suit, none were visible when he was working. Except maybe when the sleeves rode up, tattoos were often a great way to identify someone, and the more anonymously he could move through the world, the better.
He started walking through the studio to the back, where there was a door marked 'PRIVATE'.

Taylor hobbled as he realised his knee was hurting. As he walked down the middle of the client bays, he caught a glimpse of both the clients faces as he passed. Both looked shocked and confused. He was hunched over, supporting his ribs, almost dragging one foot, cuts all over his face and hands, and his clothes ripped. He must have looked like a cheese grater with all the holes he had in him.
Never mind.
Taylor walked by the small bathroom to the left of him, went through the private door, and started to make his way up the stairs to the second floor of the building.

The stairs were wooden with a carpet section running down the middle, the walls, again white, with a black handrail. It wasn't as warm, and it was more business, more professional now that he was away from where any studio clients may see him. He felt like every step took twice as long as it should have but eventually, he made his way to the second-floor landing. As he rounded onto the landing, there was only one door, also marked 'PRIVATE'. The floor and decor matched the stairs, and he walked to the end of the hall, back towards the front of the shop and rounded back again to make the climb up to the third floor.
Again, same decor.
Not for the first time, Taylor wished they could put a lift in this building. He wasn't exactly sure where it would fit, but it would be easier than having to keep walking up and down these bloody stairs.
He reached the third floor. This time, there was no landing, and the door sat flush with the edge of the stairs, leaving only a small square directly at the top to stand on and turn before entering.
This door too was marked 'PRIVATE', but also had a code pad on the wall. Very private.
Taylor entered the code, and a little light on top went from red to green, and the audible sound of a lock disengaging was heard. He pushed down on the handle and went inside. The green light above the door turned red as he did so, indicating that no one else was welcome to enter.

3

Inside the top floor was all one room. The smell hit Taylor first, a clean smell. It always smelled like scented candles or something, yet none were ever on display. Given how much smoke he had inhaled, the combination of the ink from downstairs and the scent used in this room was a welcome relief.

It had wood panelling covering the lower half of the walls, the wall joins, and the ceiling skirting. The ceiling itself was white, with what seemed to be hundreds of tiny lights in it, almost like stars. It always amazed Taylor at how bright the room was without feeling artificial and causing headaches when you spent a lot of time in there. Not that he often did, but he was grateful about the whole room not causing headaches right now. He had one that he thought was good enough without any additional outside help.

The floor was a wood effect, much like the flooring on the studio level, but this one seemed thicker; maybe it was real wood?

He had never thought to ask.

To be honest, he didn't really care.

In the sections of the walls that were not wood were painted white and held much more useful items. On the left-hand side was a wall of weapons secured behind a metal grate with a key code lock, much the same as was needed to enter the room itself, but Taylor imagined the code would be different. He had never needed to gain access to them, so he had never tried.

On the right wall were two monitors. He had used these a lot. They had access to the mainframe that he got his assignments from. They were secure. When he was first introduced to this place, he was told that nothing could hack into this room. He believed it. He hadn't been doing this much more than six or so years, but he had never heard of anyone being able to gain access to this room, let alone any of the technology that resided in it. He sometimes wondered how they did it, but it wasn't his role in The Company, so he always quickly pushed it from his mind so he could focus on his assignments.

On the walls behind him were two security monitors, each showing four different camera views, mainly of the studio, but some from the second floor, the stairwells and even some on the street showing the main and the rear entrance doors.

Straight in front of him were two more Chesterfield sofas. Almost identical to the two that resided in the waiting area two stories below, but these were a lot less worn. A lot fewer people had sat on these two. They sat under a screen that took up the entire space on the far wall. There was no white painted area around it, and again, Taylor often wondered when he first started and would walk up to the screen and sit on one of the sofas, how did they get that in here?

Not today, though.

Today, Taylor could not have cared less about the enormous monitor screen or how they kept the building secure or the code to get to all the rifles, grenades, and other assorted weapons that were securely locked away.

He just wanted to get this over with and go home.

He had secretly hoped that they would have called him in tomorrow instead, but no such luck.

As he made his way over to the sofa, the monitor flickered and came to life. It didn't display a TV show, or a film, or any form of entertainment. Instead, it was divided into a couple of square images shown at once, like if you minimise two screens on a computer and place them next to each other, but one of these just slightly overlapped the other. The screen on the left-hand side looked like a heart rate monitor you would see in a hospital, but in this case, it was flat, so it seemed as if the patient had met a sad end. Then a soft, female voice, slightly metallic-sounding given the transmission, came through the four tiny speakers in each corner of the room. Though the speaker delivery system was tiny, the voice filled the room.
Commanding, yet soft.
Deliberate, but not overpowering.
Taylor groaned as he collapsed into the seat. It wasn't graceful at all, and if anyone had seen him, seen his face, they would have thought he was dying.
It was certainly how he felt.
Taylor suspected that there were many cameras hidden in this room, but none were so apparent as to be a traditional style mounted to the wall, and he had nothing to hide when he was in here, so he didn't mind.
As the voice entered the room, the monitor line flickered to match the words and the pitch it presented.
"Good evening, Red."
"Good evening," Taylor replied; both words felt like razors across his ribs as he spoke.
"Your assignment has been completed?" It was worded as a question, but he already knew that she/they knew the answer.
"Yes," he replied.

"Primary assignment payment has been transferred to your account."
At this, the second screen showed the number rise from £0 - £20,000.
"Secondary assignment was not successful, and no additional payment shall be transferred."
"Fair enough."
"The client has requested to know why you were unsuccessful in acquiring the information they requested."
Taylor took a deep breath, "I was unable to secure any further electrical information as requested due to extenuating circumstances. The target had sabotaged the equipment as a backup to ensure that it would not be taken or accessed by anyone other than himself. I had secured a laptop that had been destroyed via a virus or a deletion code or something to that effect in the hope that the client may still be able to get something from it. However, during the events that followed, it was destroyed. I had not been given all the relevant background information and was unaware of a secret lower level basement in the property. This allowed the target to get a head start and destroy data. Things then became complicated when a bomb was activated in the property and destroyed all possible devices."
He was out of breath. Those few sentences had felt like physically the hardest words he had ever spoken. With no more adrenaline to keep him going, he was starting to feel it, all of it. He tried to find something that didn't hurt. He came up short.
"Thank you, Red. This information shall be passed to the client. Any witnesses?"
"Not that I am aware of."

"Any evidence or similar to point to The Company?"
"Maybe, I cannot confirm or deny. I was clean; however, I was cut in several places during the explosion, and there may be trace DNA at the scene. Target also caught me on a camera, but upon re-entering the building after the explosion, all the computers were destroyed. I believe it was a closed circuit, just for security. However, I cannot confirm that."
"We will monitor the situation. Is there anything else you would like to add?"
"Not at this time," Taylor answered.
"Due to injuries sustained, you are off active duty until you are sufficiently able to return. Is that understood?"
"Perfectly."
"That will be all Red. And once again, thank you for your service."
"You're welcome," Taylor said as he climbed off the seat and made his way back the way he had come, back out through the door. He heard the lock engage as he closed it. The light changed again to signify it was available, and Red started to make his way down the stairs.

Red was his designation name. Actually, it was pretty much his only name that he could remember. He had a few fake names that he gave out to people when questioned. His favourite was Logan Taylor, and that was often what he decided his name should be. It's the name he gave himself. But at work, to most others, he was Red. That was the code designated to him when he had been recruited and joined The Company (that was all he had ever known it to be called). That was why he had the red tie. It was uniform in many ways. He knew of other members like himself. He had met Agent Blue a couple of times and Agent Purple when their assignments had crossed, or it was too big a job to do by himself, but The Company had assigned them to work together at that time. Taylor knew very little about either of them personally.

He also knew of the existence of Green, Orange and Yellow members but had never met any of them. It seemed that was the way. You had your assignment; that was it. Compartmentalised, that way, should a member be caught, they could only give up so much. He didn't care. He never wondered what part he was playing in the bigger scheme of things. He didn't need to.

Taylor got his assignment. He carried it out.

During his time at The Company, he had been kept relatively busy. Most of the time, it was men in power that he was hired to remove; he assumed so someone could take their place and their power. Once, a foreign diplomat was using his diplomatic immunity to get involved in something that some other people wanted to keep him out of.

Taylor didn't know which side of the coin he was on, which side he would be considered to be on if he was in a comic book or a film. Would he be the hero, would he be the villain? Or would he be the pawn that kept getting moved around doing everyone's bidding, being used to cross and double-cross the main characters until he was killed off at the end?

Who knows?

He didn't care.

He wasn't about saving the world. He just wanted to work, get paid, and then retire somewhere isolated in a few years. Remote. Peaceful.

He had no relatives remaining. No close, personal connections, no loved ones waiting for him to come home, or that could get kidnapped to be used against him, and he would have to go and save them. No, his life was simple.
Work.
Get paid.
Retire and disappear and just be by himself.
Maybe in a few years.

Taylor reached the bottom of the stairs and walked back through the door into the tattoo studio. The studio was a front, designed to hide what was upstairs but still keep a business face on things. They probably didn't need to, but he liked it. He also got his tattoos done here, and it was an excellent way for people to meet and discuss things should they need to, and it not look too suspicious. Taylor didn't have many contacts, he didn't need many, but they would predominantly meet at the studio whenever he did. It was a safe space for the most part (depending on who was in the chair being tattooed, of course) but most people that came in knew what it was, knew what world it lived in, and the people that frequented it.
It reminded him of when he was told of the old Tailoring shops that used to be used as places for the spies during the war as they were low-risk buildings to be attacked. Taylor wasn't sure if that was wholly accurate but liked how it made him feel. Like a spy, a spy with his own secret hideout. He knew of many other buildings that housed a similar set-up for The Company's members to use depending on where they were in the country, well, the world, but he believed only this one was a tattoo studio. *Craftsman* was a

central hub, and many agents would use it. He was UK based, so that was what he was usually assigned. But The Company would often send agents overseas for assignments.
He wasn't a spy. He was far from a spy.
Also, other members used the building when they were local, so it wasn't just for him. Oh well. He still liked it.

He made his way back through the studio and pushed out into the evening. It had been a long day, and the sun was threatening to set and plunge the world into darkness.
Let it, Taylor thought. I could use a tomorrow.
He unlocked the Jaguar, once again grimaced as he climbed in and started it up. He waited for a break in the traffic. It seemed a work shift somewhere had ended as many cars driving past were driven by people with orange or yellow high visibility vests on and the same logo, although he couldn't clearly make it out or care. Once a gap presented itself, he pulled out and began the drive home, letting the roar of the engine and exhaust flush out any remaining remnants of the day. He couldn't wait to get home and take a shower.

4

Somewhere in America

The Committee all sat around a table. It was not a round table, like King Arthur's, showing that every man was equal.
They were not equals.
Yes, every man and woman who sat at the long table, all 12 of them were powerful; they all came from different fields or businesses and were all incredibly successful. Some were business owners; some were politicians, some held power in court, some in law enforcement and all had their strengths. Their reasons for being there. Their motivations.
Most of it was money. Money and the hope of raising their stock and status to even more than they currently occupied. They all wore suits. Fancy suits that cost more than some new cars, they looked just like any other gathering of business executives hashing out a deal. This was not the case, though, as they were kings of their domains.
None, however, was more powerful, more important, or more successful than the man sitting at the head of the table. The thirteenth man. Thirteen was often considered to be an unlucky number, but not for him.
The man sat in silence, looking at all the faces in the room with him, scanning everything. He was a numbers man; he knew the sanctity of checks and balances and that one slight deviation from the plan could cost millions. Billions. And not just in money. In time, manpower and all manner of other things. If he

set a plan, he expected it to be followed through. He was tall, just over six foot five, and had the figure of a man who enjoyed the finer things in life. Good food, good wine, lots of sun. His grey hair was covered in black dye in an attempt to still present as young, dynamic, and dangerous. He was in his sixties and had made a good life for himself. And money. Lots and lots of money.

He wore a deep grey suit with a faint chequered pattern, freshly polished shoes, and a power tie. He was a man who was comfortable in what he presented to the world because he was his world. He owned it, and anyone who tried to say different didn't say much for long.

He had moulded and crafted the group of people sitting in front of him, and he knew everything about each and every one of them.

He probably knew them better than their partners did. In fact, he knew he did because he knew who was cheating on their partners and with whom.

And when.

And where.

And so on, but he needed to know all this information and much more about all of them because that way, he had control. He knew what points to put pressure on to ensure that what he wanted to happen happened. He had worked his way into this position, this dominating control, this power, and he would be damned if he was going to let someone here - or anywhere for that matter - try to take it from him and take over.

He knew their weaknesses, and while he never made a big deal about it, never mentioned it, he could pressure any one of them to do whatever he wanted.

He didn't need to, of course. They all feared him. Or respected him.
He didn't know which. It didn't matter as long as they did what they were meant to do.
He wasn't the thirteenth man in the room at the head of the table. He was the first – the head of the table.
The Boss.
The Chairman.

The room was just like any other big business boardroom in any other company, only bigger. It was huge. The Chairman had once heard a remark about it looking like the kind of boardroom from a Bond film, only bigger.
He liked that. They saw him with Bond villain status. However, in the real world, he would have had Bond killed and then just carried on with his day.
The room was long and wide, like a large rectangle. From his view at the table, the right side of the room was one complete window looking out over the city. He supposed it did look a bit Bond-esque.
The walls were white, and there was a cabinet down the left-hand side that looked to hold files and on top was some discreet plants in pots.
Sat at the large, black topped table were the other twelve people. Six each side. More men than women, but more women than had ever sat here before for one of these meetings. He liked that. Equality. Almost.
He liked having women on the team. People were a lot less sceptical about women on the whole, and more often than not, a woman was able to talk her way out of most situations.
Who would have a woman as the first suspect when so many men do the same things?

But women were dangerous. Much more so than men, in his opinion. They were ruthless, just as capable and determined as any man he had worked with. If not more so.
He knew it was only a matter of time before a woman was sitting in his chair. He welcomed it.
But only once he had done what he had set out to do and not before. God help her if she tried before.
The blinds were down on the window, and the hanging lights lighted the room. There were two of them over the table, and they looked like chandeliers; the light they gave was lacking, though, as most of the light in the room usually came in the form of natural light through the usually opened window. It did however, give the room an appropriate ambience.
Everyone was quiet. A couple of them fidgeted. A couple more took sips from the glass of water that was in front of each of them.
One man looked agitated. He was uncomfortable and nervous. He should be. He messed it up. He was lucky he was still breathing.
Mistakes would not be tolerated.
The Chairman cleared his throat, and the room seemed to get even quieter at the anticipation of what was coming, even though no one was talking.
“Thank you for coming,” his accent was strong. He spoke with confidence, as if his words, even though just a greeting, were the most important in the world. In that room, they were.
Silence. Nobody spoke.
“We are convened today to discuss Geologica Industries. As you know, we want their rights. Rights that we should already have,” He paused. “But don’t.”
Silence. Nobody spoke.

A few shifted in their seats.
"What happened?"
Silence. Nobody spoke.
Then a voice, a voice that should have sounded deep given its tone yet sounded like a child who had just been caught with his hand in the cookie jar one too many times spoke. Timid. Afraid. Cautious.
"They got caught."
The Chairman took a breath, slowly, purposefully.
"Caught?" he asked. "How?"
"Police, British police, and the government found out. Stopped it. One got arrested. One escaped. Three died."
These should have been sentences, but he was delivering it as if it were a lot of short statements, almost hoping it would sound better.
It didn't.
The Chairman leaned forward, placed his elbows on the table and put his hands together.
"How?" He asked slowly.
"I don't know."
"How?" This time his tone was deeper.
"One must have talked."
"To who?"
"I don't know."
"Why?"
"I don't know why he talked."
"No. Why don't you know? The second you found out, you should have asked how did this happen? He is going to want to know, and I better have a better answer than *I don't know*." The Chairman's voice had been getting steadily louder, but now breathed again and was calm.
"I'm sorry." The man's reply was weak. He was part of one of the country's most celebrated intelligence

agencies, and now he was cowering, meek, like a child. He was trying to stay in control, but his body was betraying him. He knew this was his fault, and he knew he had to fix it. It was all over his face.
"I don't want an 'I'm sorry'. I wanted this dealt with." He was getting annoyed just thinking about how much this had cost him. How much this had held up his plan. "It's a crappy company, on a stupid floating rock in the sea! This should not have been difficult! All you had to do was blow up one small stupid building, which would have sent our message to him! He would have sold to me! How he got it in the first place is beyond me! I want the rights!" He slammed his fist down, and everybody jumped and angled their bodies away as much as possible.
"Do we have anything left?" The Chairman continued.
"No, he hadn't made it yet, and now it's all destroyed, and he's dead."
"What of the one in custody?"
A woman spoke up. She was short, with long dark hair that ran below her shoulder line. It was perfectly straight and framed her face. She was not unattractive with her features angular yet soft. She could make herself beautiful, but she didn't use her looks to gain an advantage. She used her brain. She was functional over stylish. She was more confident but still cautious of how she delivered her words. "He is currently in holding. I believe he is to be questioned again soon. My sources say he hasn't said anything yet, but it's only a matter of time. He doesn't know anything, not really. So, our exposure is not at risk. We can move on."
"I want them dealt with."

"Why?" She asked but then shrank back as she realised what she had said.
"Because I don't want any loose ends, no matter how small the thread is. And because I said so."
"I'll make some calls. I'll get it done."
"Good."
"It may take a bit of time, though."
He didn't like this, but he also accepted that things changed, events needed to be appropriately handled, and sometimes the longer game had to be played, as long as the game wasn't too long.
"OK. But I expect it to be done soon."
Pressure. Pressure meant people didn't get lax, didn't get lazy, didn't take things for granted.
"I'll be on the next flight to England."
"Good."
Most people in this room worked well under pressure. They wouldn't have gotten this far in their careers without it. Pressure to perform made people work harder to succeed. If they failed under pressure? Well, then they were no good to him.
The man who was tasked with the disruption had failed. He had been given a soft target that was just enough to disrupt and not cause too much attention. He could have targeted the main operation, but he wanted to keep the mines and the equipment in the best shape possible. He could just use them then when he had control – no point in needlessly buying new machinery and equipment when there were perfectly usable ones already. You don't get this rich by spending money you don't have to.
At this point, his phone beeped in his right inside pocket. The Chairman took it out and looked at it for a

moment. Then put it back in his pocket, leaned back in his chair and breathed deep.
“I am a patient man,” he said as he rose from his chair, “and I understand things happen. Complications arise, and issues present themselves.” He began walking around the table, alongside the unit that held the files and had the plants sitting on the top. He opened one of the top drawers and scanned it for a second before his eyes fell on the object he wanted.
“The problem I have is with the people that do not allow for the complications, do not put in an alternative plan. A backup, if you will.”
He closed the drawer; he had taken out a letter opener. All eyes were facing forward, so half of the occupants looked away from him as he walked behind them. The men and women facing him saw what he had selected, and their eyes widened; one or two even started sweating a bit.
“It surprises me that someone who sits in this room has not yet grasped that and allows rookie, elementary school mistakes when planning something that is this important. It may be a small cog, however without that cog, the machine stops. Then I have to find a new way to get the machine working again.”
He stopped behind the man he had spoken to. He had his eyes forward and had no idea the Chairman had the blade.
The Chairman gently placed the blade on the man's shoulder, almost as if he were being knighted. He wasn’t. The Chairman placed his hand on the other shoulder. The man's body went rigid at the touch, and he dared a glance out the corner of his eye and saw it. He tensed. He was ready to do, to say, whatever he had to do to make this right.

"I do not take failure lightly. I need to know that every man and woman in this room can do what I need them to, when I need them to, without question. This needs to be motivation to make sure that no mistakes are made again in the future."
"They, they wo…"
The blade entered the side of the man's neck. Cutting and slicing all the nerves, cords, tendons and whatever else was in there as it did so. Only once the blade was in up to the small round hilt did The Chairman stop, then he twisted it slightly, and the people sitting opposite could have sworn they saw him smile. They kept quiet, though. The man gargled, trying desperately to say something. Anything. His eyes were wide with shock and pain. He hadn't even been able to lift his hands to try and stop it. He just sat there. Gargling, trying to breathe, blood weeping from his mouth like it was trying to escape the body before there was not a body left for it to inhabit.
The Chairman looked at the woman right in the eye, his voice deep, purposeful as always, but with him standing over the body, still holding him upright with a blade in his neck, he was much more imposing, much more dominating. The boss.
"I was talking to you. Don't make the same mistakes. Take care of it. Don't come back here a failure."
The Chairman withdrew the blade slowly, savouring the motion and the feel, and once the blade was out, he removed his hand from the shoulder, and the man, still wide-eyed, slumped onto the table.
The woman looked at the Chairman, doing everything she could to put confidence in her voice to reassure him.
"I won't."

The Chairman walked back down the table, placed the letter opener on the unit, and just walked out. He wasn't much for goodbyes, and he had said and done what he had come to say and do. He was a busy man. Everyone in the room sat for a moment. A blanket of silence covered them. Most were looking at the body that was slumped on the table. Some couldn't look at it. After a moment, it was clear he was not coming back, so one by one, they rose and left. A group of men in disposable coveralls and gloves came in carrying what looked like cleaning supplies, placed the letter opener in a bag and began scrubbing.

They were just moving the body when the woman left the room. She withdrew her phone and dialled a number. She requested to be booked on the next flight to England and then hung up.

Then she made another call to make arrangements for the loose end that she knew needed cleaning. She then started looking at how to track down and eliminate the one that was still walking around.

She was used to risk. She worked abroad for the American government doing things that didn't exist, and no paper trail of her activities existed. She was good. That's why she was brought in. There was always a chance of something going wrong. But she was well trained, and since joining the Chairman in his cabal, she had been elevated in status. She could now pretty much pick what operations she would undertake instead of being told. The woman had never known anyone else given that luxury, and she had become a lot richer. She liked both.

She knew that failure could mean many, many bad things when she was out in the field for the agency. Capture, torture, imprisoned in God knows where forever, possibly even traded around, each place worse than the last. Possibly death.

She also knew that if she failed the Chairman, it would mean certain death. She feared failing the Chairman even more than the unspeakable other possibilities that could befall her.

The woman got in the back of the Audi. She liked German cars as the quality was superior, and she believed she deserved superior. She told the driver to take her home.

Once there, she packed a bag of just the essentials and waited until it was time to leave for her flight. While she waited, she made some calls, she hadn't been to England for a long time, but she still had contacts there that would get her what she needed ready for when she landed.

Then she started snooping around and logging into places she shouldn't be. Then she started looking.

Nobody involved had any idea of the events that had been set in motion. Or what was to come.

5

Logan Taylor pulled the Jaguar down the ramp into the underground car park. The sound amplified by the confined space, and the lights automatically activated. He navigated to the empty spot that was waiting for him. He had a selection of cars down here, he liked cars, and he liked to have a variety depending on what the occasion called for. However, he regretted the choice he made this morning.
Taylor parked up and got out, walked across the car park past all the cars owned by the other occupants of the building, hearing the final clunk of the security shutter closing over the entrance to the parking area. It was always gloomy in here with the poor attempt at lighting failing miserably to illuminate the space, and it had that car park smell of car fumes stagnating the air. He made his way to the lift, his body now had run out of biological ways of helping him with his pain, but he had deduced that nothing was broken. Just battered and bruised, but nothing some rest and some well-chosen medication wouldn't be able to fix. He entered the lift and selected the top floor. Inside the lift was night and day to the damp car park. It was clean and silver, with a waist-high railing to hold on to, chrome around the floor selectors and no floor number bulbs were out. It was well maintained with bright light overhead, and no graffiti or any part of it defaced. Taylor always knew once he was in the lift, he was almost home.
Taylor very rarely used the front entrance, even when he was walking. He preferred the car park or the rear access as it meant that there was a lot less risk of being

seen. No one knew who he was anyway, but it was tradecraft that he had drilled into his subconscious, and he was fine with that.

He rode the lift right the way to the top, the fifteenth floor. It didn't stop on its way up, so nobody else had called it or tried to enter. The doors dinged open, and he stepped out into the hallway. It was like a hotel. An expensive hotel. A thick carpet and lights mounted on the wall made the space feel brighter, more welcoming. It would only ever welcome him, though. There was only one door on this floor. One apartment. Taylor called it his penthouse.

When the block of flats had originally been built, the fifteenth floor had housed three top floor apartments - Taylor preferred to call them an apartment to a flat, he didn't know why, he just did - however, Taylor had acquired them all a few years ago and had them knocked through into one big one. His one.

It was one of the properties he owned; he had this apartment, a house in the middle of nowhere in Wales on a big plot of land just outside a village and his boat in the marina. All were brought and maintained under different names and all completely independent of each other. Initially, his boat was going to be his retirement. He had planned to move about a lot, never stay in one place for too long, and be a modern-day nomad. After a while, he had lost interest in the idea. He didn't know how to sail or maintain a boat and had images in his head of being stranded out in the middle of the water somewhere, not knowing what to do and having no help – just drifting – drifting forever. No thank you. Taylor decided he would stick to spending out his days on dry land. He still had the boat though, he had had it all refurbished, and it was a lovely thing. He just hadn't got around to selling it yet.

He opened the door and entered the apartment. Home. The apartment was laid out like a giant horseshoe, and he had entered through the centre of it. There was a small walkway to access the main space, and as he walked, the small circular lights that ran through the entire area built into the ceiling lit up above him. On the walkway walls were a couple of little screens that displayed what the camera at his door and the discreet ones at the front, rear and car park entrance viewed. He had learned a few tricks from The Company's methods.

As Taylor entered the main space, the remaining ceiling lights came on to welcome him home, it was getting dark now, and the sensor had decided the extra light was needed. The walls were white, stark white, giving an already ample space a feeling of being much more significant. There was artwork on the walls, and the entire back wall had been converted to one huge window that overlooked the water. The view was spectacular. He could look out over the sea and the beach from this window, where his boat was docked. The apartment building was practically on the beach, save for a road that separated it along the front. Just to the left of the entrance was a freestanding wall, with enough space on either side to walk around, that housed an enclosed fire with a large screen TV on the wall space above it. In front of him was an L shaped sofa with the back of the small edge facing him and the long section aimed towards the fire. How it was set up, it could be used to watch the fire, TV or look out over the beach. In the far right-hand corner, blended in with the glass window, a door led to the balcony. The floor

was wood effect and often reminded him of the studio, but his apartment had full underfloor heating and was soundproofed. There were small tables at each end of the sofa for drinks to sit, and some potted plants were on display shelves and decorated corners on the floor. There was a small table between the sofa and the fire. *Bloody coffee tables,* he thought to himself.
On the other side of the fire was a space equal to the lounge area, but this housed a large, black glass-topped dining table with four chairs on either side, he didn't need that many, but that was what it came with. There was a kitchen area on the far left side of the apartment. It wasn't big and had a breakfast bar to separate it from the dining area, but it had high cupboard storage, a built-in oven, fridge, washing machine and a microwave sat on the counter next to a butcher's block of knives. Taylor wasn't much of a cook; he usually ate out or ordered in, but the essentials were there should he need or want them. Following the horseshoe shape around the left, past the kitchen area brought you into what used to be an apartment in itself, but this one now only contained the bedroom and a bathroom. A huge bed sat proudly in the middle of what used to be the living room with a small nightstand on each side, with just a lamp on top of each one. There was a bookcase against the wall and a small chair next to the window. Taylor loved to read; he much preferred to read than to watch TV. Since he was a kid, he would always say that a book is a film for your imagination. The original bedroom had been converted into a walk-in wardrobe housing all of his suits and casual wear. The bathroom was small, basically an en-suite, with a walk-in shower, toilet, sink and not much else. It was decorated

with a grey slate effect and contrasted the white of the apartment well.
Following the horseshoe round to the right, past the lounge, brought you to the main bathroom. It had a shower area in the far corner, and a standalone bath was the pride of place in the middle of the room. There were large cabinets on the wall that housed toiletries and medical supplies. It was decorated in the same grey slate tiling that adorned the walls of the en-suite. The white of the bath and sink, along with the chrome taps, looked decadent against the slightly darker backdrop.
Taylor picked up the electronic tablet from the table, tapped a few keys and the blinds slowly cascaded down the window, removing the slowly fading day outside. A few more presses, and the fire roared into life. It didn't give out much heat, it was artificial and mainly for viewing, but he liked just sitting by the fire, reading. It was one of the first editions he had made when he had begun making his renovations. He used the tablet to dim the lights and allowed the warm tones of the fire to become the glow of a light source, the light bouncing around as the flames licked and danced. A few more keys pressed, and soft piano music filled the space, speakers were in every room, and the sound was distributed perfectly. Wherever he was, it was the perfect volume. Quiet enough that raised voices would not be required - if he ever had anyone over, but loud enough to be the background sounds of his day. With the fire and the music, his day was starting to improve, even as it drew to an end.
Taylor used the tablet to log on, and once secure, he moved his money to the different accounts. Many hidden behind three or four layers of security and different companies. He worked hard for his money; he

was not about to let someone find it and take it. He never really thought anyone would. No one knows who Logan Taylor is, but he wasn't about to take that chance.
Once that was done, he moved to the bathroom and began running a bath. He put some bath salts and bubbles in to help him relax. He then stripped off, looking at himself in the mirror. He had dozens of minor scratches across his face, hands and even his arms and legs, where the glass had shredded his clothes. He rubbed some lotion over himself to try and smooth the stinging; it helped a bit. But only a bit. Leaving his clothes on the floor, Taylor grabbed a couple of towels from the heated rail on the wall and placed them on the rail attached to the end of the bath. He moved over to the cabinet, took out some strong painkillers, went to the kitchen and washed them down with a glass of water. Then he padded back across the floor to the bathroom and climbed into the bath.
As the water touched him, it felt like it was trying to melt his skin. The water wasn't that hot, but every single cut, bruise and sore felt almost instantly worse as he lowered himself in, inch by inch. Once he was in, however, and had given the water a couple of minutes, Taylor began to soothe, and after a while, he began to relax. He closed his eyes, listened to the piano music softly serenading him and let the bath heal him. He felt like he could stay there forever.

After maybe an hour or so, Taylor had lost track of time, but it didn't matter. The bath had gone cold, and he climbed out, dried, emptied the bath and wrapped himself in a robe from the heated rail.

Everything felt much better now. He was still sore, but what he had feared may have taken him out of action for a few weeks, may now only be a hindrance.
Taylor left the bathroom, got a glass of water from the fridge that was built in to look like one of the grey fronted cupboards and went out onto the balcony. The sun had set, but the lights from the street and the houses across the bay looked like the stars above. He walked the length of the balcony, so he was stood outside the kitchen, through the glass and sat on the chair, placing the drink on the small table next to it. He breathed deep, allowing the cold air to test his ribs, sore, but much better. Definitely not broken; they had just taken a pounding. His headache had now all but cleared, and his ears were back to normal along with his vision.

By tomorrow Taylor thought, *I'll be as good as new.*

He allowed himself a few more minutes for the crisp sea air to fill his nostrils, and then he went back inside and placed his glass in the sink, picked up his tablet and then headed to the bedroom. He put the tablet on the bedside table, disrobed, used the toilet in the en-suite and climbed into the bed.

He tapped a few more times, and the fire extinguished, there was a mechanical whirring as locks engaged, and then the lights went out.

Taylor rested his head, wondering what tomorrow would bring. He found a spot that didn't cause pressure on his side, closed his eyes, and fell quickly to a restful sleep.

6

As Taylor lay in the bath soothing the tell-tale evidence of a busy day behind him, Officer Roberts' day had just started. Ok, his shift was about to begin.
He was a night officer at a police station based about an hour away, and he was due to start his shift soon. Much like most of his days on the night shift start, he dressed in his uniform, had a quick bite to eat, kissed his wife of seventeen years goodbye and went off to work.
The only difference was today, as had happened a couple of times, is that he had a message on his phone to go to a meeting at the mural before he began his shift.
When his wife asked why he was going in early, he only replied with,
"To get some paperwork done and catch up before shift starts."
She didn't question that. She probably should have, but he would have just maintained the lie anyway.
Every now and then, he would get a mysterious message on his phone about a meet before his shift. He had had three so far, all to meet up in different places. The previous times it was a mysterious man wanting information from the Police database and cases that happened hundreds of miles away, but it was a universal system and never anything classified or about a case that he knew anything about because it was on TV or anything.
Officer Roberts gulped down his orange juice, cleaned his teeth, kissed his wife on the cheek as she read an

article about something clearly very interesting on her phone, grabbed his keys, shouted bye and was out the door.
He drove his old Hyundai to the mural, parked up, and walked to the steps. He had an overcoat on so that his uniform was less likely to be seen, and he had left everything that identified him in his car's glove box. There was a breeze in the air as the sun was setting. He paced and fidgeted as he tried to keep warm, clutching his fists in his jacket pockets and trying to hug it tighter to his body. After ten minutes, he was impatient. He checked his watch; he would need to leave soon to get to work on time. Then a man came around the top of the mural and started walking down the steps. Officer Roberts knew it was him. It had been him the previous times also. He slowly paced over, and they both stood looking at the mural.
After a moment of standing in what felt to him as an awkward silence, although the other man looked calm, the man spoke.
"You have a guest at the moment."
"A guest?" Officer Roberts didn't understand. Yet.
"In your workhouse. He's not much of a talker, but it's a concern he will become one, and we need him to keep quiet."
This was confusing. Typically his interaction was a slip of paper, some case details and where to send them. Then he would receive a money transfer.
This didn't make any sense.
"I don't know what you mean."
"Benjamin Sandel."
"Sandal? Like footwear for the beach?"
"No," the man paused, "Sandel. With an 'E'"
"Oh, ok, doesn't ring a bell."

"He has been moved to holding with you, which is convenient."
Something made Officer Roberts think that there was nothing 'convenient' about it.
"He needs to be convinced not to talk."
"Ok, what do you want me to do? Talk to him? Threaten him?" This was becoming unnerving; he had gone from just taking files and information to actually now threatening a suspect. This was different. He was not comfortable with this.
"I'm not sure tha…"
"Non-negotiable." The man interrupted as if he could sense the reluctance. You don't do this, and we will ensure everyone knows what you have done so far. They may even discover some things that you haven't actually done that we can make it look like you have."
Officer Roberts' stomach both sank and rose simultaneously. Fear ran through him. He was in too deep. He knew this was too much, too far, but what could he do about it now?
Report it, maybe? But then he'll be in trouble.
Arrest the man? That was a stupid idea.
Agree to do it, then don't? Possibly, but what if they found out?
Officer Roberts was snapped back to the moment when the man spoke again. "Don't worry," he said, "all you need to do is get him to take this."
He took his gloved hand out of his pocket and discreetly handed over a small silver tin; it was smooth and felt even colder than the wind as Officer Roberts took it and placed it reluctantly in his pocket.
He hesitated, weighing up if he really wanted to ask the questions in his mind… He decided to risk it.
"What does it do?"

"It will make him sick. He will be transferred to a hospital. Then your part is done."
"Sick?"
"Yes, sick."
"How sick?"
"Sick enough that he will need a hospital."
"Hospital? But they will know that he took something, won't they? People will suspect. They will suspect me. I run the desk. I'll be their first port of call trying to find out how he took something or who gave him something."
No, this, this is a terrible idea, Officer Roberts thought to himself.
"It's untraceable," the man replied. "By the time anyone looks, they won't be anything to find. You will be safe. Just say you were talking to him, and he became ill. There will be no way they can prove it was you who had anything to do with it."
That sounded better. He would be ok.
"Who is this guy?"
"He isn't important."
"He sounds pretty important if you're going to this level to stop him talking."
The man's head turned, and his brown eyes locked onto his. Officer Roberts looked away fast.
"Do this, and you will have twenty-five thousand pounds in your account by the end of your shift."
Holy shit! Officer Roberts thought, *that's a lot of money*. They could pay debts off, or take holidays, or give it to charity. Probably wouldn't give it to charity. He was a Police Officer. He did enough to help people. Although how much help did he really provide sitting at the custody desk all night? Either way, charity would be very unlikely to see any of the money.

The man's voice broke his gaze once again and was now sounding colder, sharper than before.
“Don’t do this, and you won't have a wife at the end of your shift. How long have you been married now?”
“Seventeen years.” He replied slowly.
“Wouldn’t it be nice to make it to eighteen?”
Officer Roberts thought about this. How his wife of seventeen years, all the love, the good moments and then the fights, the ignoring him to spend all her time looking at her phone, moaning about him ‘not contributing’ and how he ‘doesn’t like her friends’. Maybe life wouldn’t be so bad on his own. Probably best not to risk it, though. May draw too much attention, and there were things he liked about her, things he loved about her, and twenty-five grand would stop her moaning for a while. He would say he won it online gambling again. She didn’t care where it came from as long as she could spend it.
He realised he hadn’t replied.
“Yes.” was all he could think to say.
The brown-eyed man turned and started to talk away.
“Message when it is done. The new contact information will be sent to you.”
Then the man left. Officer Roberts watched him go and realised how tense he had been holding his body. He was afraid. Genuinely afraid. This was different. If he were caught, it could, no, it would end his career, his marriage, or worse case, he could go to jail.
Officer Roberts walked back to his car, thoughts swirling and fighting for space in his head. All he had to do was get this Benjamin guy to take the pill. Then the man would take care of the rest. He fingered the case in his pocket.
How hard could it be?

He arrived at work on time, just, and he kept his head down, not wanting to make eye contact with anyone. He felt like all it would take is one person to look him in the eye, and they would know, they would all know. Oh god. What had he got himself into?
He made his way to his workstation. He was at the back of the police station at a desk in front of the cells. It had been a quiet day his day shift counterpart had told him and that it was looking like it would be a calm night, and there wasn't really much to do. Other than playing games on the computer.
Officer Roberts laughed weakly at this, not really listening to what was being said; he was still running his fingers around the case in his pocket. He said goodbye to his counterpart and settled in for the night. He said hi to a couple of PCs that walked past but didn't really engage much in conversation, and both times the conversation died quickly, and they moved on.
He tried to make himself look natural, yet he felt like he had forgotten how. He forgot how he sat, how he walked. It was crazy; it was like he was having an out-of-body experience screaming at himself to be normal! Play it cool!
Eventually, the station around him died out, and all the day shift stragglers staying late had gone. The PCs were out on their patrols, and the busy station's hum was replaced with a slight buzz.
He took a couple of deep breaths and thought to himself,
Now or never.

7

The cell area had no cameras other than the one overlooking the entrance. It was a dead-end, only one way in and one way out. The powers that be had decided that no more security had been required. It seems it wasn't in the budget.

There was some irony in a police station not having excellent security.

But today, Officer Roberts was grateful. He took a few deep breaths. He composed himself.

Why was he worried? It wasn't like he was breaking him out personally. It wasn't like he was actually doing anything wrong.

He knew he was. But he kept playing it through in his mind, his role was minimal, and the man said it couldn't be traced, so by the time he was examined for what was causing this sudden illness, there would be nothing to see, and he would be in the clear. It would be ok.

It would be ok.

It would be ok.

He had looked at Benjamin's file while he was waiting for the station to quieten down enough, and he wasn't even really that bad. A couple of arrests for fighting was about it. He was, however, suspected of being part of a group that had been planning to build a bomb, and involved with the man who died in a house explosion down south earlier. But it was speculation at the moment. It showed that he had been interviewed, moved up here and was due to be transferred again tomorrow. There was a note saying that a special unit

was tasked with investigating because it was related to something else that was deemed classified. Seemed a bit of a stretch.
But maybe that's why the man wanted to get him out.
Was he helping the bad guys?
Was he involved in something?
It seemed likely that he was, due to the urgency of people wanting to talk to him. Transfers usually take days to deal with, and some people were coming to collect him in the morning.
Officer Roberts kept running different scenarios in his head, and none of them were good. Yet he knew that now he was too far in, he had to do it.
He reasoned to himself that the guy had been caught once before. So he would be caught again, surely. Especially if some special unit was interested in him. Realistically he would be caught trying to escape the hospital. They may not even send him to the hospital that the man wanted them to.
But he would have done his part, so there should be no repercussions on him. He had done what he was asked. The rest was up to other people.

He had put it off long enough – time to do it.
Officer Roberts made his way down the hall of heavy blue doors with little letterbox viewpoints. All were currently closed. Most of the time, they just held vandals, drunks or people who had got a bit carried away and got into fights. Usually also drunk. He arrived at cell 4. The name scribbled on the small black chalkboard name plate identified it as being occupied by
Benjamin Sandel
With an 'E', he thought to himself.

Ok. I can do this.
He opened the letterbox style viewpoint.

8

The view into Benjamin Sandel's cell was a familiar one. A drab, dull and uninviting familiar one. The walls had started life as white, but now they were yellowy-brown, dirty and every wall covered with some graffiti.

Officer Roberts was never sure how because they were supposed to have everything confiscated before being put in the cells.

A small metal frame bed, big enough for a single person with a mattress that had seen better days and a few blankets. The blankets got washed. Just not as much as they should do. A simple silver toilet sat in the corner.

Under the blankets and on the mattress was a man. An average man. He was of average height and average build. He was white with brown eyes – currently closed, but he knew the colour from the file – dark scruffy hair and a beard. He wore jeans and a hooded top. He was in his 40's.

Officer Roberts cleared his throat.

Benjamin just laid there.

He cleared his throat a bit louder.

Benjamin didn't stir.

A brief moment of panic set over him. What has happened to him? What if the escape plan is ruined because somehow, he has died in his sleep?

Would the man deem that his fault?

It couldn't be; he wasn't there all day.
He was going to do it. He honestly was. But now he's dead, and it's all gone wrong!
Benjamin groaned.
Thank God! The relief washed over him, but then the daunting original thoughts welcomed their way back into his mind.
Benjamin stirred and rolled over. It looked like it took him a second to register where he was. Then he groaned again.
"Get up." Officer Roberts ordered.
"What?"
"Get up," he repeated. He was using his normal voice, hiding his trepidation. *HE* was in control of the situation.
Benjamin got up.
Many thoughts had gone and were still going through his mind of how to get Benjamin to trust him. In the last possible second, he decided to take a punt on the truth. Partially.
"I'm here to help get you out." Officer Roberts voice was low. There was only one other person in the cells that night. A drunk. But he still didn't want to risk being overheard.
"What?" Benjamin was still sleepy as he approached the hatch. He was taking too long to process information.
"Benjamin. I need you to focus."
"Benji,"
"What?"
"Call me Benji. *Benjamin* is what my parents called me. I hated it; they always sounded so disapproving of everything I did."

To be fair to his parents, Officer Roberts thought, *looking at you now, in your current state, your current situation, they probably had good cause to be*. He just moved past it.
"Ok, Benji. I'm here to help get you out. Take this…"
He removed the small capsule from the silver tin. It was tiny, smaller than any medication he had ever seen and passed it through the hatch. "It will make you feel ill. Very ill. But it's ok, it's meant to. I'm then going to call for an ambulance for you, and once you get to the hospital, people are waiting there to get you out."
"What? You're playing me. You just want me to tell you things. I don't know anything."
At that moment, looking at him, Officer Roberts had an overwhelming sensation to believe him.
"Look, whatever you are into, whatever you did, someone wants you out. There are people coming tomorrow to interrogate you about a man who blew up in his house today," he glanced at his watch; it was past midnight, "yesterday." He corrected. "And about others that were killed during a raid of a warehouse."
He paused, "what were you planning on doing?" He asked it as if he cared about him and just wanted to help.
"I ain't saying nothing."
It was worth a shot. Officer Roberts was aware of how long he had been talking and that while the only camera was at the mouth of the access door to the cells, it would still record how long he had been gone. This had to be hurried along. He took a chance.
"Ok, whatever, I don't care. People want you out." He said, "clearly, you are a valuable man for them to orchestrate such a plan to get you free. They obviously want you out there, helping them. They clearly aren't

disapproving of what you did; they want you back. They want your help."
The moment of truth, would he buy it?
A smile spread across Benji's face; he was running over those words in his head.
"Yeah," he said slowly, "they want me back."
Yes, he had. Officer Roberts considered pushing on who 'they' were; he was a cop after all. But he wasn't a detective. He just ran a desk. It wasn't up to him to solve this. Instead, he just pushed home his point to try and speed things along, so he said, "exactly. Now take it. Quick."
Benji put the small capsule in his mouth, flung his head back and swallowed.
They both stood there a moment. Nothing happening. Had it worked? But then Benji groaned, moaned, and grabbed his stomach with one hand, his throat with the other.
Perfect. Now all Officer Roberts had to do was act panicked, call an ambulance, and he was in the clear. This had actually gone better than he had thought it would have. He wondered why he had been so worried.
Then Benji started foaming at the mouth.

9

Benjamin Sandel, or Benji as he preferred, hadn't had a great life. Granted, it was all his own making. Drink and drugs from a young age, breaking and entering, theft. He had a couple of arrests for fighting, but that was all he had been caught on. So no real hard time. He had a kid somewhere. The mother had taken him, and he hadn't seen either of them for years. The kid must be grown now.

A while ago, Benji started running with a new crowd. His 'crew', he called it. He was over forty now. He really should be starting to get his life together instead of acting like a teenager playing gangs.
They had been approached to do a job, one of the members of his crew had once served in a bomb unit, but since coming home, he had deteriorated and taken a downward spiral. He was falling into the habits that Benji had been participating in for years.
They should have gotten him help to deal with what he had experienced. He needed it,
But they didn't.
They should have said no when they were offered a lot of easy money just to blow something up.
But they didn't.

Long story short, somehow the feds and the pigs (did people still call cops pigs? Benji did) found out. They raided the old warehouse they were squatting in and killed two of his crew. He didn't resist, they didn't have enough guns for all of them to have one each, and

Benji didn't have one, so he screamed when they burst in, and when they shouted to him to get on the floor and put his hands flat, he complied instantly. While lying there, he had been looking at the bodies of his crew members that had been brave enough to shoot back. He would avenge them.
Some detectives had questioned Benji. He hadn't said anything. In reality, he didn't know anything.
He wasn't in charge of the planning, wasn't in charge of building the thing. He was kind of just there. He was playing at being a gangster.
Later that day, he had been suddenly moved to a new station. He didn't know why, but he assumed they thought that they had better detectives and that they would be able to get him to talk. But when he arrived, he had just been put in a cell.

Now there was a cop at his hatch, waking him up.
By the end of a bizarre conversation, Benji had come to a realisation. He was worth something. The cop had told him he was going to help him escape. He was unsure at first, thinking this was just another way of getting him to talk. He wasn't an idiot. He wouldn't be fooled easily.
Now, however, he had realised that he had worth. The people who had hired his crew had obviously seen something in him, even if he didn't have the first idea who they were – and they were going to help him escape.
He felt he finally had vindication for all his choices, his decisions. This was it. Once they got him out, he would do whatever they needed. They would be his new crew. He would find Brandon, and they would carry on. They

would end up running the streets, using this as a springboard for everything going forward.
Benji had been rolling a small capsule around using the tip of his forefinger and thumb. His way out. This would simulate illness, like in the films and then they would break him out.

He put the capsule in his mouth, flung his head back and swallowed. He waited for something to happen, but for a long moment, he felt fine. Maybe it failed? Perhaps it was a trick to see if he was guilty?
Then something happened.
His stomach felt unsettled. Benji groaned, it got worse, and he started moaning. It was working, he felt like crap, but he hadn't thought it would have been this bad. Almost instantly, he felt it get worse. He felt like his stomach was on fire; he felt like he needed to vomit. He thought he was burning from the inside out.
He grabbed his stomach, but now the feeling was rising, spreading. He felt like it was seeping into every part of him and up to his throat. He wanted to scream but couldn't. He grabbed his throat, panic now raging through his body. His mind was trying to comfort him, *'it's ok, they're getting you out'*, but his body was screaming in pain.
Benji instinctively opened his mouth to speak, shout, and scream for help, but no sound came. He realised he was foaming at the mouth; saliva was dripping, and his airways were becoming blocked.
He couldn't breathe.
What was happening?
Help. Someone help.
The cop was just standing there. A look of disbelief on his face, and as Benji's airways started to restrict, he

sank to his knees. Now Benji couldn't even feel his stomach. Blood was pumping to his brain; he tried to gasp for air but failed. Both his hands were now clutching his throat. His brain was shutting down, and he could hear his heartbeat in his ears and yet couldn't feel it pumping anything around his body.
A lifetime of bad decisions flashed before his eyes. Regret. His parents were right about everything. Benji decided at that moment, even if this were all part of the way of getting him free, if he suddenly woke up and people were trying to help him escape, he wouldn't. He would stay. He would tell the police what he knew. Take his punishment. Then he would find his son, apologise to his ex and work at being the best dad and human he could be. He would turn his life around.
As he fell from his knees and then onto his back on the floor, his vision started fading, a black circle slowly closing his field of vision. He saw a figure, blurred, rush to him, kneel next to him. He was saying something, but Benji couldn't make it out.

The last thing Benji saw was the light on the ceiling of his cell. For a moment, he thought it was the light at the end of the tunnel he had always heard you saw when you died. Heaven?
But no. It was just his brain grasping at the hope that this might all be ok.
No. The last thing Benji saw was just a bulb. In a dank, crappy cell that could have been avoided.
He was a disappointment.
The last thing he saw was that light. The final thought in his mind was reserved for his son.
The things he should have done. The things he could have if he'd been given his time again.

The things he would have if he had made it through this.
The last thought, the thought of his son, slipped away, and Benjamin Sandel 'Benji', died.

10

What was happening?
Officer Roberts couldn't read minds. He had no idea what Benji was thinking, the stream of thoughts racing through his mind.
He just stared at the man, grabbing at his throat, gasping for air with his eyes wide. Fear and panic like he had never seen before.
Then he dropped to his knees. Then his back.
Then Officer Roberts reacted. Fumbled his keys, his hands starting to sweat. He ran into the cell, knelt beside him, and started telling him he would be ok.
He was trying to reassure him.
But Benji was dying.
Officer Roberts got up and ran, sprinted down past the cells to call an ambulance. He no longer needed to act the panic as he had planned. He was panicking. He was scared. This was not supposed to happen.
By the time he returned to the cell, Benji was dead.

Once Benjamin Sandel's body had been taken away, Officer Roberts knew it was over.
There would be an investigation. That was a given. He may lose his job. He may go to jail.
He sent a message to the details he had been given, he had explained that Benjamin was dead, and he was now waiting for the reply. What would they do? Would they blame him? Would they kill him? It had been an accident.

Then a notification pinged up on his phone, it caught him by surprise, and he jumped. It told him that he had just received a payment transfer of twenty-five thousand pounds.
He had not expected that.
All he had to do now was pray that the capsule was indeed untraceable, get through the investigation, and then maybe retire from the force and try something new.
Benjamin was supposed to have been sprung free. His death, however, had also ended Officer Roberts career. Benji was not supposed to have died.

Benjamin Sandel had died precisely as planned. The man who had given Officer Roberts the capsule sent a message confirming the death. Then he just put his phone back in his pocket, walked over and sat back down on the sofa, took another sip of red wine from his glass, and carried on his conversation.

11

The following day Taylor awoke feeling refreshed. He felt much better than he had expected to and welcomed the new day.

He got up, threw his robe on, used the toilet, and went into the kitchen. He poured himself a glass of apple juice from the carton in the fridge and took a sip. He used the tablet to open the window blinds, and the sun streamed in, introducing him to the new day. He stood for a moment at the window and looked out over the water. Then he finished his drink, went back through the bedroom to the walk-in wardrobe room, selected some running clothes, a long sleeve t-shirt and joggers to make sure his tattoos were covered and placed them on the bed.

Every morning Taylor liked to exercise. Either run along the beach or swim. He didn't fancy salt water in his cuts, so he opted for a light run this morning. He went to the main bathroom, took a few more painkillers, and wrapped a bandage around his ribs. Then he cleaned his teeth, got dressed and went for a run.

He left via the back entrance and jogged a few buildings down. He would enter the road from behind a different building each time, so it was hard to pinpoint which one he actually came from and crossed the street and down the steps onto the sand.

It was a warm but overcast morning. Great weather for a run. He did a few stretches and started jogging at a

steady pace, wanting to check how his body would react before he pushed it.
The sand was soft and golden, the waves crashed against the shore, and the salt air filled his nose. Taylor loved that smell. There were a few other people on the beach that morning. Some were fishing further down, and a couple of joggers were keeping pace with each other, deep in conversation.
It would get busier later. Once the sun had burned through the clouds, everyone would be making their way to beaches.
He liked it early in the morning. It was quiet. He never listened to music as he ran as he wanted to hear what was going on around him.
He did a couple of lengths jogging, and once he was happy, Taylor picked up the pace a little and then a little more, stopping just before he was at a full sprint. He ran a few lengths like this, and when he stopped, he was drenched in sweat. There were patches under his arms and across his chest and back, which was starting to soak through his bandages. He doubled over, his hands on his knees and panted, breathing in deeply, sucking as much air as he could into his lungs as the sweat started to sting.
Once he was back in the apartment, Taylor stripped off, put the clothes in the washing and took a shower. Once fresh, he had some breakfast. Sausages, bacon, scrambled egg, beans, and toast. He put the empty dish and cutlery in the sink. Then he picked up his discarded suit from last night. It was ruined.
That was disappointing, but it wasn't the end of the world. He had many suits the same, all made to measure for him, but he still hated when he had to throw one away.

He had a housekeeper that had been provided and vetted by The Company. She would come in, keep the place clean, and dispose of his waste. All his rubbish was taken away and incinerated. He removed the SIM card from his Sony Xperia, snapped it in half, dropped it in what remained of the apple juice in the glass, then fished it out and threw it away.
He went into the walk-in wardrobe and opened a small box that sat on one of the shelves. He selected another SIM card and placed it in his phone. It powered up. He knew his phone was secure - all his transmissions and details were - as long as the little green padlock symbol was displayed. But he felt happier changing sim after every job.
He would have disposed of it last night, and should have, but it slipped his mind.
He dressed in a white t-shirt and jeans, returned to the living area, and turned on the news.
He was curious if anything had been reported about the house explosion.

...Still looking into what happened here, on this street. It looks like a gas line explosion that has taken the life of the occupant. No one else seems to have been injured during the blast that took place here yesterday, and investigators are still looking into what caused it. It is thought...

Taylor turned off the TV and picked up his tablet. He searched a few different sites, and they all seemed to suggest the same thing. If there had been anything left behind to link him to what had happened, The

Company had done a great job shutting it down and removing any involvement.
As he was skimming other news articles, he glimpsed one regarding a man who died in police custody overnight. Investigations were ongoing, and there wasn't much more information given, so he moved past it.
He closed the tablet, leaned his head back to rest on the back of the sofa and took a minute to listen to the waves.
Taylor had decided that he would go into work today and declare he is available to be put on the active list. He only got one or two significant assignments a year. Most of it was little stuff, small jobs that would only take a day or so, nothing that would really push him. He would get assigned two or three of these a month – like the Houton assignment. He was aware any bigger jobs would probably be given to another agent, and he was happy with that for the minute. He was never bothered by doing the smaller jobs; most agents hated them and only wanted the bigger stuff, but he didn't mind, and he was more than capable of any small assignments while he finished healing up.

After a few minutes, he got up and changed into his black suit, black shirt, and red tie with a silver tie clip. There was a whole shelf full of watches. Many different makes from across the world, and as with his clothes, he liked to think he had a watch for any occasion to match his wardrobe's attire for any occasion. Taylor considered a watch to be the ultimate men's wardrobe accessory, and very rarely was he seen out without one unless he was exercising. Then he had

one that monitored heart rate and all sorts, but he didn't always use it.
Taylor rarely used the watch he had been given as standard issue when he joined The Company, and today he selected a black leather strapped Bremont with a white dial face. He preferred leather strapped watches to the stainless-steel bands, as he thought they rested better on his wrist, so he normally saved his stainless-steel Omega, Rolex or Breitling models for formal dress wear.
He strapped his watch on.
He loved the feeling of his suit. It made him feel complete. He felt more at home dressed like this than he did in his leisure wear. Some men would just wear a suit, and it seemed like they were suffocating, but when Taylor wore a suit, it looked like he belonged in it.

He knew he wouldn’t be at the studio long; it would take all of a minute to declare he was available, but he still liked to dress presentable. He was, after all, going to work. So he should dress appropriately.
He thought about taking the F-Type but decided against it. It was covered in dirt and debris from Brandon’s front wall, and it needed cleaning. So he picked up the keys to the Alfa Romeo. A four-door saloon car would be perfect today.
Taylor left a note on the board asking if the Jaguar could get organised to be cleaned, slipped on his Converse shoes - he wore formal when needed, but for day-to-day use, he valued comfort and manoeuvrability - and left the apartment.

He rode the lift down to the parking floor, and the door dinged open. Taylor stepped out and walked through the parking lot to his allocated spaces. Among the line-up was a deep red Alfa Romeo Giulia - it had a fancy specification name, Quadrifoglio, but he couldn't pronounce it - what he did know is it was powered by a twin-turbo 2.9 Litre V6 engine derived from a Ferrari. He preferred his Jaguars, but he liked this car too.

He unlocked it, climbed in, started it up and made his way out of the garage.
Before he set off for the studio, he had to make a stop, it wasn't far out the way, and he knew it wouldn't take long. He pulled up outside a Tailors shop. It looked like a simple shop. The building was white with dark wood window surrounds, and a sign above that was green with gold letters saying:

THOMAS ANDREWS
MASTER TAILOR

There were mannequin busts on display in one of the windows showing off some fine dinner jackets in various styles and colours. There were also beautiful, elegant women's dresses on full display in the other. Taylor got out, walked up a couple of steps to the shop door and entered. The shop was quiet, there was no music playing, and it smelt of new clothes. It wasn't a smell he particularly liked when it was this strong, but whenever he opened a new suit bag, he would take a deep breath and let the aroma fill his senses.
Inside the shop was beautiful. It was deep green and white coloured with beautiful deep coloured wood shelves and units displaying ties, tie pins, pocket

squares, and other accessories. There were displays of shoes in different styles, from formal dress to oxfords and shoes with decorative pattens across the toes called brogues. A large sofa was in the middle of the waiting area, and a portfolio of different suit styles sat on a table next to it. Suits were hanging on pegs, ready to sell in various sizes, cuts, styles, colours, and patterns.
A man came down the stairs, and a smile spread across his face when he saw Taylor. He was an elderly man; he had thin grey wispy hair that went in all directions and was wearing a grey suit with a faint pinstripe pattern that looked like it fit like a second skin. It fit his body perfectly and moved in unison as he strode across the shop floor. Most men Taylor had seen of Tom's age were hunched over and looked frail, but Tom was striking in his health, and he carried himself with an air of distinction that Taylor admired.
I hope I can do that when I'm his age, Taylor thought.
"Red," Tom said, "how lovely to see you."
"And you, my friend, and you."
They embraced in a hug, and once they separated, he looked Taylor up and down, admiring his work on the suit he was wearing.
"Tom," Taylor began, "I need a new suit."
"Of course, my friend, what do you need?"
"Same as usual, but I'm thinking white shirt for the next one."
"Ok, ok", he said. "When would you like it by?"
"Whenever is convenient. I'm going to be in town for a while, and if anything comes up, I still have some in the wardrobe. I just like to keep on top of it."
"I understand," he smiled, "this way, please."
Thomas Andrews, or Tom, as he preferred was in Taylor's opinion one of, if not the best tailor he had

seen or worked with. He held him in the highest regard and nowadays would trust no one else with his suits.
They went back to one of the fitting rooms, and Tom got out his measuring tape and did the routine of measuring all the areas he needed to ensure a perfectly fitted suit.
Once it was all done, they returned to the front of the shop.
“Give me a call when it's ready?” Taylor asked.
“I’ll have it delivered to your apartment, sir.”
“Thank you, Tom, and stop calling me sir.”
“Of course, sir,” Tom replied, a sly smile across his lips. Taylor smiled back, left the shop, got back in the car, and headed towards the studio.
It was a short drive over with minimal traffic, but when he arrived at the studio, the parking out front was full, so he pulled into the car park around the corner and walked back around and into Craftsman Bespoke Tattooing.
The shop was empty. One artist was sitting at the back at a table drawing something, and he looked up briefly before turning his attention back to his work.
Taylor walked straight through the shop and through the far door marked private. He made his way up the two flights of stairs - remarking how much easier it was this morning - although he was sore enough not to get too carried away with himself. Once he reached the top floor, he saw that the room was vacant, so he entered the code, and when the lights changed, he entered. Although the room indicated its availability, a woman was standing at one of the monitors on the left side of the room. She turned when Taylor entered, and he hesitated and paused before she beckoned him in.

She turned and moved to one of the sofas in the middle of the room. She was wearing a black knee-length skirt with a white shirt and a black tie. She had blonde hair tied into a neat ponytail and artwork on her nails. Her legs had tattoos of flowers and mandala artwork flowing down in perfect unison to her figure. They looked like they had always been there and grown with her. She sat, and Taylor walked over and sat opposite.
"You know," she began. She was very softly spoken but not mousey, she could still be heard, and Taylor did not doubt that she could control any room she stood in front of. "I had a feeling I would be seeing you today."
"Did you?" Taylor replied. "I do work here, you know."
"Yes, but I knew you wouldn't be coming into work today. I felt you would be coming up here and talking to her." She motioned her head to the screen behind her that had a wavy line voice displayed last night as it talking to him.
"Oh."
"Yes, to tell her that you are ready to be put back onto the active list," she paused, "after one night."
"Maybe I just wanted to see you."
"Did you?"
"Always."
"Liar."
"I can come here for two reasons."
The sparring of the back and forth of the conversation had only taken a moment. It seemed as soon as one finished, the other spoke; it was like a verbal tennis match. But now Taylor stopped and turned his tone a touch more serious.
"It wasn't as bad as it looked." He tried to sound reassuring.

“I’m sure it wasn’t.” A small smile escaped the corner of her mouth. She got up, walked over, and picked up a tablet. She started using it as she walked and sat back down on the sofa.
A moment later, she looked up at him.
“Done.” She said, “but don't think me an idiot. You will be on light work until we see fit to change it. And you can work downstairs if you so choose.”
“Thank you.”
“Anything else?”
“Just one last fleeting moment to look at you.”
“Goodbye, Red.”
“Goodbye, Administrator.”
As The Administrator got up, Taylor did the same, allowing her to leave the conversation first. He walked back to the door and shot a glance back, but she was already back at the monitor, continuing with whatever she was doing before his interruption.

Taylor walked back down to the studio; the artist was still drawing at the desk. The shop was still empty.
The employees of the studio, and The Company in general, wore black and white. The only real colour came from the tie that each active member wore.
The staff, including the artists, housekeepers, and even the administrator, wore black and white. Sam was once again dressed in all black with a white tie. He had close-cropped hair, dark eyes and was clean-shaven.
“Hey, Sam,” Taylor said.
The artist - Sam - looked up. Taylor didn’t know Sam’s last name.
“Red.” Same greeted.
“Busy?”

“No more or less than usual,” Sam got up, and they both walked over and sat on the Chesterfield sofas at the front of the shop.
“See you had an eventful day yesterday, given the state you were in when you traipsed through here.”
“Yeah,” Taylor’s hand instinctively reached across and touched his side.
“I'm thinking of getting a memento.”
“Yeah? What are you thinking?”
“A cartoon bomb.”
Sam smiled, “Yeah, is that what gave you that ass whooping?”
“Partly, a guy helped.”
Sam smiled again, “Where do you want it?”
“Right arm. I’m thinking with a smiley face.”
“Done. You working?”
“I have just been up and declared myself available and put back on the active list but was told that I won’t be getting anything juicy for a while. But they did say I could still work down here. So at least it gets me out and working for a while.”
“So, I get to see your face more.”
“Lucky you.”
“So, when do you want this new addition added?”
“Whenever. Maybe sometime over the next few days. I don’t see anything exciting much happening.”
“Done. See you tomorrow for work?”
“See you then.”
They both raised from the sofas and walked in opposite directions. Sam went back to the far end of the studio and carried on with his work while Taylor left the shop into the sunshine. It had started to burn through the clouds, and the temperature had risen. He walked back to his car and drove back to the apartment.

12

The flight had taken what felt like forever. England was a long way away, and while the woman didn't hate flying per se - she was a first-class kind of girl - it just seemed like a lot of dead time.

She had, however, been very productive. She had received word that the custody problem had been resolved and that just left the last piece and the cop to deal with. The cop would be easy, but a man was running around with a little bit of information in his head, like a headless chicken. There was a man out there that knew something. Not much, granted. But something and that was too much. He had to be removed from the playing board, and she was not prepared to mess it up.

During her searching and after getting in touch with specific contacts she had, she discovered that the police had no involvement in the incident that ended with a house being destroyed. That had been a third party, outsourced by government agencies to keep their hands clean and their involvement limited.

It turned out that it was meant to be quiet and that there were other things in play here. Things that would have led back to her, the cabal, The Chairman.

So really, it was a good thing that the government investigation was dead in the water.

The woman had been given a name. Details for an outfit called 'The Company'. She was sure they were not supposed to be divulged, but what's the point in having contacts if they don't tell you things. From there, she had delved into and collected all the data she

could from anyone who knew anything and eventually, she had everything she needed to make a start.
She still had a problem, though, the headless chicken variable.
But a thought had struck her.
An outside party may just be the perfect way to deal with it.
While she had contacts, people were already looking for him, and she needed him gone first. Fast. She also had to make sure that she could keep her hands clean. She needed to be the puppeteer of the situation. She needed a puppet.

She got her phone and dialled a number.
The Chairman answered after the fifth ring.
"Yes."
She filled him in on what she had found and proposed her plan.
"We get this third party to deal with the wondering variable. And from what I have found, they offer many services, so, if they prove competent, we could use them to intimidate the old man. Make him sell without drawing any attention to ourselves. Minimal risk. It could all be done within a few days. Providing they are competent."
There was silence on the phone. She knew she had been sent to do it herself, and with enough time, she would be able to track him down and deal with it, but how long would that take?
From what she had heard, their technology would mean that they would be able to find him fast, and if needs be, all she had to do was follow whoever they sent. Even if they couldn't live up to what she had

heard, she would have eyes on the target and could take over.
In her mind, it was a win-win.
But *her* mind wasn't the one making the decision.
"Ok. See how they do. But whatever the result, I hold you responsible." The Chairman
The line went dead.
A moment of doubt entered the corner of her mind. She pushed it aside. It would be ok. She would be there in case anything went wrong. It would be fine.
She made the call.

The woman had remembered almost instantly why she hated England when she had landed. There was something about the air, the way it smelt maybe, that irritated her. And they drove on the wrong side of the road. And their accents. Many Americans loved the British accents, all high class and posh sounding with their fish and chips, their scones, and their cups of tea, but not her. Then there was the weather. It held off today, but it rained so much in this country. Awful. She hated it. She couldn't wait to get this over with, get back on the plane and get home. She decided to give herself a week. She wouldn't allow herself to be here any longer than she needed to be.
In her mind, she wouldn't be caught dead on this floating rock. When the Chairman had been making his derogatory statements towards this place, she had agreed with everything he had said. But needs must. At least she wasn't here forever.
When she had arrived, there had been a car waiting for her, a Black BMW 5 series. In the boot were cases with some essentials, this included weapons. It was illegal to have guns in England, another reason she didn't like it,

but there were more black-market ways of getting them than people realised. It was quite easy to lay your hands on firearms here.
The woman's had come courtesy of one of her contacts. They were black market, but not the usual cheap, unreliable crap most people had here. These were what their government agents and security services would be issued along with some machine guns and grenades. She had no idea what she would do with grenades, but anything was welcome.
The BMW came with GPS - or Sat Nav - as they called it. Once she had finished making the calls she needed, she plugged the address in, weaved her way out of the airport, constantly reminding herself to focus on driving on the right side of the road.
The groundwork had been laid. All she had to do was follow and make sure it all went to plan.

13

Taylor had only been back at the apartment a few minutes when his phone pinged. He picked it up and looked at the message:

New appointment available. Would you like to take it?
Yes / No

That was fast, he thought. He hadn't expected anything for at least a couple of weeks. He sat on the sofa, logged on to the tablet and waited for the little green circle to load in the bottom left corner. Once it completed its circle, a small green padlock symbol appeared in the centre, and he logged into his account. There was only ever basic information relayed through this because while it was secure, there was no point in tempting fate. It stated that an assignment was available that was related to his previous one. While it was a new client, there was already a large amount of information available, and it was deemed the *lowest* risk designation.

Easy work. Something simple to get me back into it, Taylor thought. *Why not? Worth a look.*

He responded to the request, logged off, picked up his keys and left the apartment less than ten minutes after walking into it.

The bonnet of the Alfa Romeo was still hot. It hadn't sat idle long enough to cool itself yet as Taylor once again brought it to life and eased out of the garage.

He arrived at the studio for the second time that day, parked in the car park around the corner and once again

entered the studio with his arrival announced by the small ding of the bell over the door.
Nothing had changed since he left except that now a man was sitting in the chair and Sam was tattooing. He gave a cursory glance as he entered and then went back to his work.
He walked through the shop, through the door, up both flights of stairs. The room was vacant, so he entered the code and pushed the door.
The Administrator was still there. She looked like she hadn't moved since he had left, and when she saw him enter, she closed down the screen of what she was doing and silently walked past him and out of the room, giving him a small welcome smile as a greeting as she did so. No words were spoken.
Taylor sat and faced the screen. As soon as the Administrator had left and the locks had engaged, the screen erupted into life. Once again, there was a small square in the top left-hand corner, the green heart line flat. The square next to it showed a mugshot of a man that Taylor recognised.
The line moved, and the slightly metallic woman's voice entered the room.
"Good day, Red."
"Good day."
"A new assignment is available, and as it is related to your previous one, I saw fit to offer it to you first as you are now back on the active list."
Taylor nodded. No words were required.
"This man is Todd Bartlett. As you know, he is an associate of Brandon Houton. You came across him during your research phase of your previous assignment. A client has contacted us and has taken out a contract with regards to this man.

Before I go any further, would you like to know more about the assignment?"
"Yes, please proceed."
"Very well. The client has requested the termination of Todd Bartlett. To be effective immediately. Would you like more details?"
"Yes."
"Very well. The client requests that the termination looks like an accident. No traces must be allowed. They have requested an accidental death, a hit and run or a physical attack. However, there must be no chance of subject survival. The client has agreed to the price of this level of contract, and the deposit has already been made. Is that understood?"
"Yes, completely," Taylor answered.
"Are you happy to accept this assignment? If you feel in your current condition, you are unable to do so; it will be reassigned to another agent."
"I accept."
"Very well. Please see the monitor for your documents. They have now also been downloaded to your Company tablet. For any further information, please see Edgar. The client has requested to know the time window for the completion of the contract, so please inform the administrator before you leave."
Taylor nodded as again no words were required.
"That will be all, Red. And once again, thank you for your service."
The monitor turned black, and Taylor rose, adjusted his suit, and left the room. Typically, with a new assignment, Taylor would spend a bit of time at the monitors gathering any information that the Company had been able to ascertain about the contract, but he had already done all the leg work on this one. All he

needed now was a place to start. He thought he already knew where it would be.
This wouldn't take long.
Taylor left the room and walked down the stairs to the second-floor landing. The Administrator stood waiting. He opened the door and walked into what Taylor called the Tech room. There were walls of monitors, and it was filled with the sound of whirring machines and devices.
The room was bright and felt open, but the air smelt close in here. There were artificial air vents, but it was a busy room, lots of body heat.
There were five stations set up in here, and each operator wore the same outfit as Sam, all black with a white tie. All of them were typing away, some on desktops, some on laptops, some on tablets. At some point, Taylor had worked with each of them, depending on what he was doing and who was free when a new assignment came. Today he was working with Edgar.
Edgar was three stations down, and he looked up when he saw Taylor approaching.
He only knew Edgar by his first name, if that was his name.
Most members of The Company only had one name.
"Red," Edgar greeted him as he approached.
"Ed," He replied.
"I heard you were out. Then very quickly back, and now you're back on assignment."
"Crazy couple of days."
"What do you need, man?"
"Location on my target."
"Ok," he dragged out the word as he typed. "Looks like the bar."
"That's what I thought."

"Think he's done an all-nighter, I have him entering with three others yesterday, but nothing of them coming out," he typed a few more keys, confirming what he had said. "I don't have eyes inside, though."
"Ok. Thanks, Ed. I'll call if I need anything."
"No problem, my man. I'm here for all your enquiry-a-tive needs."
"Is that a word?"
"Sure, why not." Edgar beamed.
At that, Taylor left, and Edgar went back to typing.

Outside the second-floor room, the Administrator was still waiting.
It's incredible how still she stands, Taylor thought, *especially in those heels*. She smiled and tapped her tablet.
"Do you have a time frame for completion?"
"Oh, get my stuff, an hour or so to get there, a couple of hours to find the sweet spot. Say four hours."
"Thank you."
"You're welcome."
"Good luck out there."
"Thank you."
Taylor walked down the stairs and back through the studio, the bell signalling his departure. He walked round to the car park and drove home, thinking to himself how easy this would be. All the leg work had been done already; this was just a case of sealing it all up.

Once back at the apartment, Tayloe changed. A suit would stand out a mile in the bar he was going to; it was a dive. He dressed in a black long sleeve t-shirt, grey cargo trousers and grabbed his leather jacket and cap from the cupboard. He then went to his weapons storage and selected a switchblade. He had decided that a mugging/stabbing would be his way today. He had watched the group a lot when he researched Brandon, and Taylor knew that Todd liked to go out the back of the pub and smoke. He was the only one who did, so a stray mugging/stabbing would be great as the dark alley would conceal the act. The client hadn't requested the body hidden, so removal wasn't an issue. That made things easier – just a random, careless, senseless act of violence.

Taylor folded the blade away and slipped it into his right pocket and his phone into the left. Once again, he grabbed his car keys and rode the elevator down for the third time that day, walked through the car park, and drove the Alfa Romeo out of the garage.

14

The drive was uneventful. The sun was in his eye line, and he had to put his sunglasses on, but it was another lovely day, summer was approaching, and the weather was getting people ready. The roads were relatively clear, and other than a small stop in traffic, it was a clear route straight through.

The only thing that Taylor thought was of note was that there was a black BMW that kept appearing in the rear-view mirror, catching his eye.

He thought nothing of it: busy roads, lots of black BMW's around.

15

The American woman hated this. She hated driving in this country. She couldn't seem to navigate on this side of the road and make it look natural. The car felt different, bigger, the blind spots seemed enormous, and she always thought she was too close to the line and ended up swaying. A few people had beeped their horns at her already, but she just carried on driving. She didn't care that they didn't like it; they didn't matter. All she had to do was keep following him. She was confident he hadn't seen her, though. If he had, he had made no reaction to try and evade her.

16

Taylor drove slowly past the White Lion public house that sat on the corner. It was quiet, still too early for the after-work crowd. It wasn't a nice place, and nobody would go in there for a meal.
It had dirty green faded paint on the walls, and the window surrounds were wood that had chipped, broken and fallen off after years of onslaught from the weather. No care had been given to this place in a long, long time. The sign was worn and faded, and there even looked to be tiling missing from the roof.
He had first discovered it when looking into the Brandon contract. He and all his buddies would frequent this place regularly. Taylor was pretty sure they were the only people that did.
He thought the place looked like it wanted to be a bikers place, but even the bikers had decided it was too bad.
There was a public car park a few streets over, but Taylor slotted the Alfa Romeo into a side street alley much closer. Once he was done, he just wanted to get out.
A black BMW drove past the mouth of the side street, slowed, but then sped up again and was lost to sight.
Taylor checked he had everything he needed. It smelled like garbage. He was parked on an access road for waste collection and emergency services, and there were wheelie bins full of rubbish lined up down the wall, backing onto the rear of the businesses that held property along the main street. Taylor got out of the car, grabbed his cap and jacket from the backseat,

slipped them on, locked the car up and started walking.
As he walked, he dialled Edgar. The little green padlock appeared, and then the phone started dialling. He answered almost immediately.
“What’s up?”
“Is he still in there?”
“I believe they are, haven’t seen anything to say they have left. But I don't have eyes on the back alley.”
“Ok.” Taylor hung up.
As he approached the bar, Taylor saw a black BMW turn onto the street, pull in and park badly a few buildings down over the road.
It was probably just paranoia, and he needed to keep focused on what he was about to do.
The door to the White Lion was just as shabby as the rest of it, and Taylor had to put effort into opening it. It squeaked as it finally submitted and granted him access. Inside was, if possible, worse.
It was dank, and most of the lights didn’t work. The floor was sticky, and it looked like the tables were too. They were traditional pub tables and chairs that you had to climb up onto. The space wasn’t big enough to have actual tables to sit and eat at, but it did have a pool table. It was the only thing in the pub being used, and four people surrounded it, two leaning against the wall drinking while two played. The players' pints were on the table at the end, waiting for them.
Every step he took, Taylor could feel his boots sticking to the floor. But this was part of the job. He had to be a chameleon, fit in anywhere, and today was this tiny, horrible pub. As he moved around the bar, he looked for cameras while keeping his head low so the cap

would stop them from seeing him if there were any. Unsurprisingly – there weren't.
"What you want?" The barman asked, his voice old and croaked as he spoke.
"Pint," Taylor answered.
"Of what?"
"Whatever's cheapest."
"Fine."
As the barman shuffled down the bar to get a glass, Taylor made his way to the bathroom, passing the men around the table. He recognised Todd instantly and was grateful that he wouldn't have to go looking for him. He opened the bathroom door and then regretted it as the smell hit him. He raised held the back of his hand against his mouth and nose. He checked for any exits as he knew of the front and rear doors but wanted to check if someone could escape through a window or something. They couldn't; they had been painted shut many years ago and were too small to be able to force a way through.
Taylor came back just as the barman finished pouring the pint. A lady was now sitting in the far corner, as far away from the group at the pool table as possible. Taylor took his pint, paid, and sat in the middle. He had a clear line of sight to both doors, the group at the pool table and the woman from where he was.
He turned his attention to her.
She looked pretty. Her face was angular yet soft. She had what looked like a small amount of makeup to highlight her features, but it was dark in the pub, and he couldn't make out more. He did, however, notice that she shouldn't be in here. Her clothes were too nice, too expensive, and while she was wearing a few layers, tight black trousers, jumper, and a big overcoat - it

looked like she thought it was going to be a lot colder or she was used to being a lot warmer - all of which looked out of place in here. Taylor knew it sounded bad, but she looked too good for this place.
He was trying to work out why she was there when he heard a loud wolf whistle come across the room. The four men then made their way over to her, forming a semi-circle around her and not leaving her any way out.
This had taken a turn.
Taylor could hear them asking her questions, and he hoped she would just leave, and everyone would go back to what they were doing because then maybe Todd would go for a smoke. Possibly his last one.
When it became clear that they wouldn't leave her alone, he knew he would have to intervene. Not to save her or anything as stupid as that, he just needed them to go back to their routine.
He quickly formulated a plan.
Then he stood up, made his way over.
"Excuse me. I think the lady would like to be left alone." He said. This got their attention, and they all turned.
"What you say?" One said, apparently the leader, but not Todd.
"Leave her be. C'mon."
"No, we'll leave her be when we're done, mate."
"I'm not your mate." Taylor countered.
"What? Think you can talk like that to me, do ya?"
Taylor had slowly been moving towards the door, drawing them away and allowing the woman to leave. Which she did, but not as quickly as he had expected. He thought she would have practically run out, but no. She calmly got up, picked up her bag and left.

This irritated the talking man. Taylor could see it coming. The fight. But he needed to avoid it. He didn't want too much attention. He needed them back in their routine. He knew what he would do.

When the first punch came, Taylor let it hit his jaw, but he rolled his body to match it, so the impact was low and nothing to be concerned about. Yes, it hurt, but all punches hurt. What was more important was to make them think it hurt more than it did, which was easy. He doubled over, raising his hand to his face, trying to amplify the pain for the spectators. Then like a wounded animal, he cowered over to the door, leading them to hopefully believe that one punch was enough, and then he left.

Outside he could hear cursing coming from inside as they yelled profanities at him. He then straightened up and walked around the back of the pub and down the alley. Even at lunchtime, it was overshadowed and plunged into darkness by the backs of the taller buildings around it. Perfect.

Taylor put his gloves on, and he waited.

And waited.

And waited.

Would they go back to their routine? Had that woman blown his chance? He was just formulating his next move when the back door swung open and there, in all his glory - Todd Bartlett.

Todd had his head down and was lighting up a cigarette. He took a couple of drags and turned his back to where Taylor was waiting. The door of the pub clicked shut behind him.

Taylor slowly crept up behind him, watching where every step went, taking his knife out and drawing the blade.
Then Todd put his cigarette in his mouth, unzipped his jeans and began urinating against the bins.
Taylor was so close now he could smell the cigarette and see how it illuminated his face as he took a drag. Every sense was on high alert, waiting to issue the abort sign to his body. This was riskier than he would have liked, and he could think of many better ways of doing this, but sometimes the simple way is best. This was more likely to be successful than a car crash where he had a chance of walking away. He could find faults with the other ways too. Hell, Taylor knew he could find faults with this way too.
Todd could turn.
His friends could decide to come out.
Someone could walk past and spot him.
Many scenarios of this going south played through Taylor's mind, but he kept his body trained, alert for any of them while he executed his play.
The moment came with no abort warnings registering in his body. Taylor couldn't see anybody around to be a witness; he couldn't see anything or anyone that may discover them.
His hand went over Todd's mouth, suppressing any screams and forcing the cigarette inside as the knife went in like it was butter, penetrating his clothes, under his ribs, into his organs. Again. And again. As his body died, he was still urinating, his body expelling fluid that would never be replenished. He laid the body down, and just to make it look more random, Taylor stabbed a few random wounds into his torso. He then took his wallet and his phone, slipped them into his

cargo pockets, retracted the knife's blade, and put it away. Ready to be cleaned when he got home.
No one had seen a thing.
Then he put his hands in his jacket pockets, pulled out his phone and waited for the little green padlock, dialled, and began the short walk back to his car.
The black BMW was still poorly parked on the opposite side of the street.

17

As Taylor walked, he checked in and reported that it had been executed as planned, that he would be returning for debriefing, and he would be there in a couple of hours. It had been a much better day. After the exploits of the last assignment, this was just the way he needed it, almost like a palate cleanser. It had gone off without a hitch, really, except for the woman. Something in the back of his mind was itching him; *why was she there*? There was something Taylor couldn't put his finger on.

It was probably nothing. Just a woman in the wrong place at the wrong time. Other than that, though, it had been perfect. Taylor had fulfilled the contract. He had not been spotted, and Todd's friends probably still think he is just out having a smoke. By the time they realise what has happened, he will be long gone. Taylor doubted they would call the police. But even if they did, it had been clean, and there would be nothing to trace back to him.

The sun seemed to feel a little bit brighter, a little bit warmer now as he turned down the alley where he had parked.

A man was sitting on the bonnet of his car.

He looked like a reject from a gang film. He wore baggy trousers, a tank top with an open hoodie that looked two sizes too big and more gold chains around his neck than looked comfortable.

Before he had taken another step, Taylor knew what was going on. This was about to be an attempted carjacking. So much for a sunnier, brighter day.

As he slowed his pace, he felt more bodies appear. There were four in total, all dressed pretty much the same, there must have been a sale or something, and all looked like they were spoiling for a fight. They looked like the kind of men that were used to getting what they wanted just from saying it – letting the threat of violence be enough to scare people into doing what they wanted.

Taylor wasn't intimidated. He didn't scare easy.

He did, however, curse himself for parking where he did. It was a rough area, and he thought that parking it somewhere as he had would remove unwanted attention and make it easier for him to blend in and come and go unseen. It turned out the Alfa Romeo may as well have had big neon signs pointing to it.

As Taylor neared the car, the men seemed to encircle him. He had expected this and didn't mind it, but he usually preferred to have everyone trying to harm him in front of him, in full view, where he could keep an eye on them.

"Gimme them keys, man." The one who was sitting on the car said.

Taylor slowly looked around, not making eye contact, he didn't want them provoked, but he was discreetly eyeing each one up. He didn't have time for this, he needed to put as much distance as he could from here and from the body laying a few streets over, and this was going to make it difficult. He needed a quick resolution to this.

Typically, if you take out the leader of a group, usually the one who runs his mouth all the time and likes to stand in front of the victim to be the big scary man who runs things, then the pack falls away pretty quick. It was just an unspoken rule of gang mentality. They always saw strength in numbers, in their bosses, but you take that away, and they usually scamper pretty fast.

"I don't want trouble," Taylor said.

"There won' be any if ya 'and over them keys to my new ride."

The man sounded like a rubbish extra from a TV show that really needed a script rewrite. Taylor was also pretty sure he saw a gold tooth in his mouth.

"Just let me be on my way. No one needs to get hurt."

Taylor had now loosely raised his hands, bent from the elbow, so they level with his shoulders, fingers slightly curved, a show of surrender. But he had no keys in his hands.

"An' ya won' be if yah 'and them over."

The circle took a step closer and closed in around him.

The Alfa Romeo had an electric start. This means it started by pressing a button, and the key fob was just an oval thing that locked and unlocked it. In one of the keys, there was an emergency key blade, like cars used to have, in case the battery died and you needed to get in. He didn't have that key with him, though.

For the second time, Taylor cursed himself. He would like to have a key blade right now as he could slip it between his fingers in a fist, and you have an instant knuckle duster.

Taylor had the knife still in his pocket, and he was grateful now that he hadn't tossed it, but the second he took it out, they would have jumped him. He would save it as a backup or if the opportunity to get it out without compromising himself presented itself.

Most people, when they have a weapon, any weapon, want to use it first. It gives them power and reassurance, but a lot of the time, if it's not already in

your hand, retrieving it provides the enemy with vital seconds to gain the upper hand, even if the enemy was this bunch of incompetent idiots.
The man ran his hand along the car's body.
“Keys. I wanna take my new ride for a spin.” The man stepped close, cocking his face to the side, giving a sly half-smile exposing his gold tooth and opening his eyes wider than they needed to be, all this giving him his scary, intimidating face.
“You don’t.” Said Taylor.
“Keys, or you’ll be leavin’ in a body bag.”
How disappointing an end of all this would that be, Taylor thought. All the things he had done before The Company, all the things he had done *FOR* The Company, only to have it all ended here, in this alley, at the hands of this wannabe.
As the conversation had slowly been making its way to its climax, of which Taylor knew they wouldn’t just let him get in his car and drive away, just as much as he knew he wouldn’t be giving up his keys, he had been working.
Taylor had been studying each man, whether they were right or left-handed, which foot they preferred, if they had any noticeable weak points, a bad leg or didn’t put pressure on their body in a particular place.
He knew the conversation was pointless, but he needed to gather and correlate information. He had done so now, enough to be getting on with anyway and he mentally prepared for what was to come next.

The man with the gold tooth in front reached out his hand to grab his jacket, and Taylor grabbed his wrist, yanked him forward towards him, ducked under the outstretched arm and turned, bringing the arm of the gold-toothed man with him. Now he was facing the three remaining men. Taylor had the man's arm outstretched in front of him, and the man bent over in front, his arm in a lock, and him trying hard to keep the cries of pain inside his body.

Taylor applied a small amount of pressure, and gold tooth grimaced and dropped to his knees. The three men looked at him, not sure what to do, and Taylor made a point of looking at each of them individually in the eye, mentally naming them one, two and three while giving them a chance to leave.

But they were nothing if not loyal, and even though they looked bemused, they all stayed.

"Fucking get him." Gold tooth ordered in a strained voice through gritted teeth.

Great, Taylor thought as they advanced on him. He twisted and broke gold tooth's wrist, and a cry of anguish finally left his body. Then Taylor kneed him in the head, knocking him out, the cry stopped, and he slumped to the floor.

Hopefully, that was enough to stop the others.

It wasn't.

They hesitated but continued to advance, and it seemed they still believed in the safety of numbers. Three against one. Ok.

Taylor backed up, and they followed. He led them behind the Alfa Romeo as once this was done, he wanted to drive straight out and put distance behind this whole thing.

"You can leave now, guys; no one needs to know."

They kept coming – worth a shot.

They seemed reluctant for anyone of them to go first, and this was taking too long, but now Taylor had time to retrieve his knife, he extended the blade. The blood

on it caused a reaction, maybe enough for them to leave.
No, no such luck. Taylor turned the handle in his hand, so he held the knife backwards, so the blade was now coming from the bottom of his fist. This allows his hand to still punch with the bonus of the blade should he need it. Or want it.
Ok.
"Then let's just get this over with," Taylor said.
They seemed to hesitate, then number two came at him, followed by three, one held back.
Two swung a right-handed punch, and Taylor ducked; he could have stabbed his leg but resisted and just delivered a punch to two's side, sending him reeling and crashing against one of the rubbish skips. He turned his attention to three as he lunged with a right hook, this time Taylor grabbed his wrist with his left, stopping the swing, lashed out with his knee to three's stomach, causing him to bend forward and then moved in close and brought the blade down into his right shoulder blade. His scream echoed through the alley; this may have been a mistake.
Taylor withdrew the blade from three's shoulder and glanced at the mouth of the alley; then, he turned to check the other. Nothing. Two was up now, and one was still circling, keeping just out of reach. Taylor turned as two lunged at him, tackling him to the floor. Taylor fell and rolled, got a bit of distance as two lashed with a kick that missed its mark.
Once they were both up, two came again, with another kick. Kicking was great in films and a scrap, but like this, it puts you off balance. Taylor caught the kick, bringing it close to his body, two was now only balanced by one leg. Taylor went low, dragging the

blade along the inner thigh of the only support two had, not deep enough to do any real damage, but the sudden pain and shock were sufficient for two to arch back and to cry out, and his trousers became wet with blood as it began running down his inner leg. Taylor kept his momentum, turning two around and gripping him in a headlock, his cries stopped as his airways became crushed, and he passed out after a couple of seconds. Taylor let the body drop, and it thudded to the ground. Two down. One to go.

One had produced his own knife; it wasn’t anything exceptional, and Taylor was pretty sure it had come from a kitchen set, but a blade was a blade and could always do damage. While it may seem like a good idea, usually going up against an opponent with a knife while holding one yourself was normally best avoided. Yes, it's always nice to have a weapon, but then up against someone with one, whether they are trained or not, his experience taught him to have both hands able to be open, the risk of defence was greatly increased – and you could always disarm and use the opponent’s knife against him.

Taylor retracted his blade and put it back in his cargo pocket, the blade now having taken trophies from three people that day. He readied himself for the attack. However, one was reluctant. So, he had to press the issue. Taylor moved in, and in a defensive move, one jabbed the knife out. It was instinctive and had no real thought or power behind it. It was easy to counter.

He grabbed one's wrist with his left hand, used his right to put pressure on his elbow bend causing the locked arm to give way and then all he had to do was guide the knife, still held by its owner, into his own body, causing him to stab himself in the side. Instantly,

Taylor raised his right hand to cover one's mouth before he could make a sound. His eyes wide, as if his body couldn't work out what had happened; he was stabbing someone, so why was he in pain? Before his body could figure it out, he had passed out.
Taylor, who had once again moved into a choke hold, let the second body he had passed out that day drop to the floor. He checked how his body had dealt with it, his side a bit sore still, but he hadn't taken any hits, and it felt good. Adrenaline does most of the work at the time, and it's more often about checking in with yourself afterwards and making sure everything's still ok. But he felt good. He felt like himself again, and as long as he could babysit himself for a few days, he would be good as new.
Taylor moved the bodies between the rubbish skips, so it was unlikely they would be found before they woke up. He emptied their pockets, threw their phones in one of the skips and kept their cash.
He didn't think the wounds he had caused were fatal, and they would be ok if they got treated once they woke up.
If they weren't, well then, they should have walked away.
Taylor made sure he had left no obvious evidence behind, as with Todd's friends, he didn't expect these guys to call the police, but just in case.
He then unlocked the car and got in, removed his gloves, started the engine and began the drive home. The alley incident had only taken a few minutes, but the holdup had still annoyed him. Taylor was so focused on this that he didn't see the black BMW pull out a few cars behind him.

18

The woman had entered the bar - or 'pub' short for Public House - as they called it to find it only contained a bartender and four men playing pool.
She had been following him all the way here; it was easy. His car was ostentatious, flashy and loud. She saw him turn down an alleyway and almost followed him until she saw him become stationary, then she had sped up and circled round a few streets down and came back around in time to see a man walk up the street and look to be entering the bar – Pub.
He seemed to be looking at her, and she thought he had realised what she was doing, but she pulled her BMW in further up over the road and planned to get out and just walk somewhere random until he thought she wasn't important.
It turns out it wasn't needed. The man looked but then carried on. He entered the bar – Pub.
The woman got out and crossed the street. The door was heavy, but with a bit of force, it opened with a creak. She went inside.

Good God, this was horrible.

She had dressed for colder climates, and outside was bearable, but inside, it was like the sort of place that souls go to die.
She hated this country.
The bartender was pulling a drink, and she sat on the nearest stool by the door, she didn't want to as it looked disgusting, but she needed to sit somewhere to be less

noticeable. The bartender looked up, expecting an order, but he just carried on pouring when she didn't give him one.
The man who she believed she had followed came out from around the back, the restroom maybe. He saw her, but then he just paid for his drink and sat down against the back wall. He put his head down, but at no point did he take a drink, not a sip.
He was wearing a black t-shirt, a black leather jacket and a cap low over his face, and he had a couple of days' worth of stubble on his face. It was still short and, from what she could see, suited his face. His grey cargo trousers looked to be holding a knife, but it would be easily missed unless you knew what you were looking for.
She knew what she was looking for; This was the guy.
Then she heard a loud wolf whistle from across the room, and the four men approached her.
Damn it.
No reason to worry.
"What's a fine girl like you doing in a place like this?"
"Thank you." The woman smiled back.
"What?"
"Thank you for the lovely compliment. I was supposed to be meeting someone here."
"Well, I'm here, and I'd certainly like to get to know you better." The man moved his hips slightly as he said this, and the alcohol on his breath was overpowering. That and the cheap aftershave he was using. Or maybe it wasn't aftershave. Perhaps it was just him.
Maybe it had been a mistake to get this close. Maybe she should have stayed outside. The woman wasn't afraid, though, and she could see Todd; he was standing over to the side, not saying anything.

She considered just killing everyone in here and then just walking out of the bar and the problem being solved – Pub, not bar.
Then the man that she had been following seemed to appear and was trying to diffuse the situation. Why? Maybe he wanted her gone so he could do what she had planned, kill them all and be done with it.
Maybe he was trying to be chivalrous and protect her? She didn't need protecting from these, or anyone by him.
One of these men had caused a lot of problems, and his friends, especially the leachy one, could just die for the hell of it, for the inconvenience.
In any case, it was time to go. But she only went when she was ready and on her terms. She lazily got up, picked up her bag and left.
Once outside, she hid and waited. She was waiting for the crashing to start, and she could see it in her head:

Pub fight goes too far, and man is killed.

But instead, the man from The Company just left. With nothing but some shouted swears as a keepsake.
What was his deal?
Then he moved to the back alley, crouched by some trash and stopped.
He couldn't see her where she was. He wasn't looking for her; he was looking for someone else.
After a while, he skulked forward. His movements were reminiscent of a big cat in the wild out hunting prey. The woman moved for a better position and saw everything.

Todd had been killed with a precision takedown. It was actually quite impressive and beautiful to watch. She realised she was smiling.

She moved back as he left the alley, using his phone. She got back in her car and waited for the red one to emerge from the alley and the cat and mouse game to begin again.

It didn't; maybe she missed it.

She got out and walked carefully to where she had seen it park, glancing around the corner before entering. The car was still there, and so was The Company man. Along with four others.

She couldn't be seen but could see everything. After a minute or so of talking, the fighting started. It was impressive. The Company man moved with conviction. Like chess, he seemed to be moves ahead, even against multiple men. His training seemed similar to hers. Maybe her doubt had no grounding.

Maybe this man could be used to help push things forward.

As he cleared the bodies, emptying their pockets and moving them, she left and moved back to her car and waited. The contract was fulfilled, and her phone pinged from a private number, saying that the deal was completed and for the transfer to be made. She transferred the money. Best money she had spent in a long time. He had done what she had asked and proved he was more than capable.

Shortly after she had made the transfer, the red car appeared and drove off. She set off, tailing him once again.

He had passed the test.

19

The death in the cells happened in the early hours that morning, and there was already an investigation set up and committees to find out what had happened.
Officer Roberts just had to keep to his story and get through this, and then he and his wife, his wife of seventeen years, would move and start again. Maybe get a little shop somewhere.

However, Officer Roberts would not be allowed to retire and just move on. He knew stuff, and he had to go. The brown-eyed man who had given him the capsule knew this and was not surprised when people higher up had given him his orders.
Officer Roberts usefulness, and therefore time, was up.

20

Driving back down south was dull, the woman thought. It was mostly highway driving - or motorways as they called them here - the weather was holding into the afternoon, and she was more confident in her driving now. More used to driving on this side of the road, the other side of the car, and was much more able to navigate the English roads. She was able to keep much further back but still keep track of The Company man.

She worked out the time difference to America as she made the call. It didn't matter; she had never known to ring the Chairman, and he be sleeping, no matter what time it was.
Did he sleep?
Irrelevant.
The Chairman answered on the third ring.
"Yes."
"The deal has been completed. No additional complications."
"Good." His voice was louder and somehow even scarier coming through the car's built-in phone speakers. He sounded like he was all around her at the same time. She was glad he couldn't see how uncomfortable that made her.
"And what of moving forward with the old man?"
"I believe it should be a go."
"Then do it but be reminded that I hold you responsible. Make sure, one way or another, it gets done." The Chairman asserted.
"Yes, sir." The woman replied.

"Inform me of when it's done."
"Yes, sir."
The line went dead as he hung up, and the woman carried on driving.
As they neared, she veered off and drove back to the hotel she had been set up in. It was nice, posh. Lots of white, cream and chrome fittings, but she still didn't feel comfortable; she wouldn't until she was back home.
A few more days, she told herself.
A few more days.

She then began the next stage of getting home, which was getting the man to sell Geologica Industries. She made the call and set the contract.

Part Two

21

Taylor's debriefing back in the room on the third floor of the studio had gone as expected. The payment had been transferred, and there were no complications.
It was only as Taylor was returning to his car, parked in the car park around the corner, that his phone pinged.
Taylor didn't have many friends, or any as far as he could remember, or many acquaintances that would often message him, so he usually took it for granted that it was work when his phone went.
This time was no different.
The circle completed, then the little green padlock appeared, and once he was back sitting in the car, he opened it up.

New appointment available. Would you like to take it?
Yes / No

Already? Strange. Taylor thought. It was average to get two assignments in a month, so it was very peculiar in the space of a day.
Curiosity got the better of him, and he was a man of work. If work presented itself to him, who was he to turn it away?
Taylor left his car and walked back round to the studio.
Agents were told to use the front door to the studio where possible, it was more suspicious to see people come and go through the back door, and with the artists

wearing similar clothes, when an agent arrived in their suit, it would not look out of place.
The usual ding of the bell.
The usual casual glance up and then away of the artists working.
The climb up the stairs up to the third floor.
The entry of the code.
Taylor once again entered the room. No Administrator was present this time, and when he sat on the sofa, the screen lit up. Once again, the line danced and peaked as the slightly metallic voice of the woman spoke all around him.
"Good day, Red." The metallic voice welcomed.
"Good day."
"A new assignment is available, and you have been requested. It is an intimidation contract. Would you like to know more about this assignment?
"Yes."
"Very well. It is with regards to one Maxwell Carson. Head of Geologica Industries." A picture of Maxwell Carson appeared on the screen.
"Never heard of him, or them, what do they do?" He asked.
"Our information shows that they are a drilling and mining company and have contracts mining and excavating at various sites around the world, including oil and diamonds, amongst others."
"Strange." Taylor said, "I thought it was normally the big American companies that got the main joy of storming through other countries to export things and get rich. But I could be wrong."
"We have no opinion on that. Would you like more details?"

Taylor knew that The Company was neutral and if he was honest, as long as he got paid, he didn't particularly care whose dirty work he was doing. He had long since passed that point. In a part of his mind, Taylor believed it had happened way before he joined The Company.
"Yes, please proceed."
"Very well. The client wants Mr Carson to sell Geologica Industries to him. However, Mr Carson has been reluctant. They would like you to change his mind."
"Why me?" Taylor inquired.
"You have been requested."
"Any ideas why?"
"It seems that it is due to the Todd Bartlett assignment. It seems the client was happy and has recommended us to be used by another party. Would you like more details?"
"Ok. Yes. Proceed."
"The client would like the contract fulfilled within a week. It will require travel to the midlands. The client is happy for you to use your discretion regarding how you would like to ensure Mr Carson signs over his company. The client has agreed to the price of this level of contract, and the deposit has already been made."
"Who wants to buy it?"
"That information is irrelevant."
This job came from the Todd Bartlett assignment, and the Bartlett assignment was directly linked to the Brandon Houton assignment. Was it related to them? Or just word of mouth, as so much is in this world?
A thought entered his mind.

"Did the client on the Bartlett assignment drive a BMW, a black one?"
"That information is irrelevant and unknown." The voice answered.
"Does this new client drive a black BMW?"
"That information is irrelevant and unknown."
"Ok."
"Would you like to accept the assignment?"
"Yes. I will need time to get my things and travel, but it will be done in the requested time frame."
"I shall relay that to the client. Please see the monitor for your documents and the relevant information we have has been downloaded to your Company tablet. For any further information, please see Edgar. That will be all Red. Thank you for your service."
Taylor moved over to the monitors and looked at the available information. There were details on Maxwell Carson. He was a short, plump man who reminded Taylor of a clean-shaven Colonel Sanders. In the pictures, he wore suits, mainly tan with an open-top button and no tie. There were also pictures of him relaxing in his garden and out shopping. There was his home address and the address of Geologica Industries main office. There wasn't much to go on, so some watching and following would be in order to find out when and where would be best to approach.
Taylor left the main room, went downstairs, and entered the second-floor room. Edgar was waiting for him.
"I got bored on that last one," was Edgar's opening statement.
"Didn't need much. All the work had been done before; it was a clean sweep."

"Nice," Edgar raised his hand for a high five. Taylor didn't. "Man, you gonna leave me hanging?" Edgar waited a beat, then reluctantly put his hand down.
"So, what you need?' He grumbled, like a child who wasn't allowed an ice cream.
"You have the new assignment file?" Taylor asked.
"Yeah."
"I need eyes on his house, his work and I need to know where he likes to go, what he likes to do, who he likes to do it with and what he spends his money on. Any vices, people or weaknesses that I may be able to use."
"Got it. I'll send whatever I find to your phone. When do you leave?"
"Once I have showered and changed. It's a four-hour drive, but I'll drive up tonight and get started in the morning."
"Cool, man."
"Thanks, Ed."
"No worries," Edgar raised his hand again for a high five. Taylor just turned and walked out. "One day, you will!" Edgar shouted as the door closed.

Taylor drove home, and once he was in the apartment, he started preparing. The apartment looked exactly as he had left it; the housekeeper hadn't been in yet. The dishes were still in the sink, and the shredded clothes still waiting to be burned. He took out his knife and placed it in one of the plastic bags from the kitchen cupboard The Company had provided him with and sealed it up. They looked like the evidence bags you would see on a police show, but they did the job. It was left in the designated box, meaning it would be cleaned and all traces removed before being brought back to him.

Taylor then stripped off, removed his bandage, and tested his ribs with his fingertips. Tender. But they would be fine.

He showered and shaved his beard back to only a day's worth of growth. He then dressed in jeans and a polo shirt, put on the same Bremont he had worn earlier and started packing.

He packed a couple of suits and some casual wear. He was wearing his boots, so he packed his Converse and filled a bag with weapons from the cupboard. Taylor had a go-bag always ready with the essentials of travel, and the only things he added were some bandages and some medicine. Just in case.

He made sure he packed for any deviation within the parameters of his assignment. It would be a simple job. Once he knew the best place to isolate Carson, it would only take a couple of minutes to convince him.

He looked at the time and planned his course.

He then left the apartment, rode the lift down and entered the parking area. He loaded up his luggage into the boot of his 4x4, a Jaguar F-Pace SVR. It was fundamentally a 4x4 version of his F-Type, except this one was black. He wished he had a red one to match, he had brought this before, and he always had black cars. Never mind. It was still good for a long while yet, and no point in changing it just for the sake of it. Taylor rarely used vehicles provided by The Company; he preferred to use his own.

Once his gear was loaded, Taylor climbed in and started it up, the echo amplifying the supercharged V8's growl, and he began his next journey, heading four hours up to the midlands.

Once he was out of the city and onto the main motorways, he put the big Jaguar into cruise and settled down for the ride.

22

The woman had left the hotel shortly after her arrival. She had gone to her room, packed, checked out and left.

Maxwell Carson's contract had been organised, and her business in the Southwest of England had concluded. All the participants of the bombing plan had now been removed from the board. The previous failed attempt had been dealt with, and now it was time to move on and make sure that the mistakes were not repeated.
She already knew most things she needed to know about Maxwell Carson. She had her contacts get her all the relevant details. She knew where he lived, where he worked and where he liked to spend his free time. Geologica had a few other small units, but they were low-level, and Carson rarely visited any of them. It was only a matter of time before the man from The Company did the heavy lifting. Her role was merely a safety net. She felt she could probably leave now and that it would all be done, but she had no intention of ending up with a letter opener in her neck, so she would stay and see it through to the end.
She had been driving for a while and would shortly arrive at the house another contact had set up for her to use. It was only a short drive from there to Mr Carson's house out in the countryside.
It required a longer drive to get to his office in the city, though.

Only a few days to go.

23

The journey was pleasant enough. The weather held, and for the most part, the sun was behind him, so Taylor didn't have to contend with the sun glare on the glass. He left his sunglasses on, though – It was just easier than keep putting them on and taking them off as and when he needed to.

He only made one stop. He didn't really need it, but as he wasn't going to be beginning the reconnaissance stage of the assignment until the morning, he saw no reason to push himself. Taylor stopped around halfway in a lovely little service station that was styled like it was an old wood cabin, only much larger. It was a much more pleasant visit than just a regular petrol station with a takeaway chain attached at the end. There was a little café with wooden tables and chairs, a small magazine shop, and some restroom facilities. Taylor saw it as a perfect time to use the restroom, and then he sat down in the café and had a toasted sandwich, ham and cheese. It was ok, and a can of coke. A bit of sugar to push him through the rest of his drive. He paid and then made his way back to the car. He stopped at the next station to top up with fuel. The Jaguar didn't need it. But he wasn't sure when he would have time to do it once he got there, so he thought it better safe than sorry.

Once he was back on the road, Taylor called Edgar to make sure his accommodation was ready. They had small safehouses in most of the cities and larger towns in England and around the world. They were never anything much, usually just a cheap flat, but it was always somewhere to put your head down and plan. It was enough for Taylor.

After another two hours, he arrived and pulled up outside his new home. It was as he pictured it, a block of flats down a backstreet in the city centre.

It was ok.

It would do.

Taylor parked the Jaguar in the space reserved for Flat 5 and went inside. He had learned to never take things straight inside a place you had never been before, even a safe one provided by The Company because you never knew if someone had found out you were coming and had planned a lovely little welcome surprise party for you. In that case, the last thing you needed was your hands full and no way of protecting yourself.

He unlocked and opened the door to Flat 5, which was situated on the second floor. An old worn carpet with cigarette burns and questionable stains, probably blood, led him to the front door. It was a black door with the paint peeling off to reveal that it had once been blue with a chrome 5 hanging in the top centre. One of the screws had broken, and it hung crooked. Taylor placed his hand, ready to withdraw his weapon and carefully pushed it open, ensuring nothing was attached to the door. The block of flats was dingy; they looked old and had seen better days. It wasn't much of a stretch to think that the only people who actually resided here

full time were people who had a penchant for narcotics and people who made their money on their back.
It didn't matter to Taylor, of course, live your life however you want; as long as they kept out of his way, he was ok with whatever you did behind your own closed door. Who was he to judge?
The flat was small, and other than the bedroom and bathroom, the whole place could be seen from the front door, and what he saw didn't fill him with confidence about hygiene. There was an old cloth sofa that was sagging in the middle, worn and dirty. There was an old TV on a low cabinet against the wall next to the door. The kitchen tops and appliances were white but looked like putting food on them would mean a possibility of death once ingested. The carpet was brown, as was the sofa, the curtains and the lampshade that covered the bulb of the free-standing lamp in the corner of the room. There was a mould patch in the top corner of the wall where it met the ceiling above the lamp.
"Home sweet home," Taylor muttered to himself. He quietly closed the door, and once he was out of the view of anyone that may have seen him on the landing, he took out his gun and stalked to the bedroom. It took him seven steps. It was a small flat.
The bedroom was much the same affair as the living and kitchen area. Brown carpet covered the floor, turning up in the corner at the edge of the room. A double bed with old brown covers waiting to welcome the next occupant. He was not keen to oblige, but it

would do. It was functional and would be perfect for his needs over the next couple of days.
The bathroom was a pleasant surprise, though. Yes, it has mould and damp, but the actual shower looked clean, and the toilet was surprisingly spotless. Taylor thanked whoever had last been sent here and promised himself if he ever found out who it had been, then he would buy them a drink. Hell, he would buy them drinks for a month.
Once his checks were done, he retrieved his stuff from the boot of the Jaguar, brought it up and placed it all on the bed. It took a couple of trips to get it all, and once it was all there and accounted for, he locked the door and called Edgar.
"Sup," was Edgar's answer.
"Edgar, I received the preliminary docs, thank you,"
"Welcome."
"What do we know of the patrol habits of his ground staff? how many, and what access points does it have available to me at the house and the office."
Taylor had already pretty much ruled out the office, too big. Too many people. Being on the top few floors up meant limited escape. And if he approached Carson there, then Taylor knew he would have to go down at some point, and he would undoubtedly be blocked. Then he would have to fight his way out, and that raised more problems than it solved.
"I have been watching and, from what I can see as you have been making your way downtown, driving fast," he lapsed into a song beat at the end of the sentence but then focused himself up again. "I think your best bet is

the house; it's a two-storey, it has lots of rooms though, gated drive and enough space for you to be seen coming, but it's when he is most vulnerable with security."

Taylor nodded, "Ok."

"I have found a couple of units that he has on file, hidden under a couple of different names, but they are definitely something to do with him. It May be worth looking into these first; may be quieter? Although I don't seem to be able to find much that he has visited these recently, if at all."

"Ok, worth checking." Taylor reasoned, "I may be able to cause a reason for him to go to one, you never know. Better to have too much information than not enough."

"Cool. Anything else, mi amigo?"

"No. Actually yes. Find out if he has a basement. Or anything that may not be on the current plans. I don't fancy a repeat of last time."

"No problemo, I'll hit you up soon."

"Thanks, Ed."

"Anything for you, and you still owe me a fist bump."

Taylor hung up. He considered driving over to the house and scoping it out, but it was getting dark, and he was starting to feel tired. He would do it in the morning. A night wasn't going to make a difference, and mistakes were made when you were tired and not on top of your game.

It could wait.

Tomorrow Taylor would start his recon. He would also check out those industrial units that Edgar had said about; they weren't on the original documents he had

been given. Edgar had done some digging and found them. They may be interesting.
Worth a look.
He looked around the flat again.
Then Taylor turned the TV on, grabbed his cap, put on his jacket, left the flat, walked down the stairs and out of the building. He did a short walk around, making sure he knew the entrances and exits, double-checking he hadn't missed any. Then, in the dusk light, he set off looking for a place to eat.

He found a café. About a twenty-minute walk away. He had passed other places to stop, fast food places and bigger chain establishments that would have done the job fine, but they had cameras, and there was no point risking when you don't need to.
The place Taylor had found looked like a small, family-owned place called *The Star Palace Café.* It was painted baby blue with white detailing around the doors and windows, and it had signs in the windows with the specials it was promoting. It also had an A-frame board out the front welcoming customers to come inside and try their coffee. Apparently, it was *'the best for miles around'*.
But best of all, there were no cameras. There was nothing on the wall, and as Taylor did a test walk past, he saw no signs of any inside either.
Looks good, he thought to himself and went inside. As he entered, he did a relaxed look around, as if admiring all the pictures on the walls. It was hard to see the blue paint due to all the pictures. There were images of

cities and landscapes all around with inspirational quotes and feel-good statements plastered across the front. He recognised many of these places from his travels and work prior to joining The Company. There was a twang of his heart as he realised how much he missed foreign travel. Nostalgia was a bitch.
What Taylor was, in fact doing was looking for any security or cameras he may have missed.
There wasn't any.
The layout of the café was simple; there were tables down the middle that were bolted to the floor with chairs attached to them, unable to be adjusted and a couple of booths along the far wall. These reminded Taylor of cheap versions he had seen in American diners.
It was a cute little café, though, and he moved to the counter. There were only a couple of people sitting at tables; a couple were deep in conversation, and a guy sat by himself, cradling a coffee and in deep concentration to whatever was happening on his phone. No one gave Taylor a second glance as he walked past. He liked this place, and as he looked at the menu over the counter, next to it was a sign saying:

We are watching you, smile for the camera.

There was a smiley face next to it, but it was for show, to make people think they were being recorded. If they had cameras, they were better hidden than most serious security nuts Taylor had come across in his time.

He scanned the menu, waited for someone who worked there to appear. There were raised noises out the back, through the kitchen. One was a woman's, and she sounded distressed. The other was a man's who wasn't happy with something the woman had done. The voices raised higher, and Taylor heard her say, "*Just leave me alone*", to which the male voice replied by saying she would regret this; then he cursed at her, and after a minute, he heard a door slam.

A woman came into view; she looked dishevelled. She was barely eighteen and looked like she had been crying, her eyes were puffy and red, and she tried to hide her sniffing as she came back out front. She had her head down, and her shoulders were slumped. She looked defeated about something. It didn't take much to work out that it was whoever the guy was.

When she saw Taylor, her whole demeanour changed. She stood up, tried to wipe her face subtly. Failed. Then said in a soft, polite voice,

"Hello, welcome to The Star Palace Café. What can I get you?"

"Are you still serving food?" Taylor asked.

"We are just closing the kitchen down, unfortunately, but we do have a couple of things left available."

"What do you have?"

"How does ham, egg and chips grab ya?"

"Sounds good. Can I get a glass of apple juice and a tap water with ice as well, please?"

"Sure, ice in the apple juice to hun?"

"No, thank you."

"No problem, it will just be a few moments for the chips. Take a seat, and I'll bring it over to you."
She smiled at him as if he was the most special man she had ever met. She was polite and good at the job. Taylor liked her.
Taylor sat down at a table that gave him a view to the front door and if anybody came in through the back. He was under a massive picture of the New York skyline and some posters about local services that people were offering.
Then he got up. Walked back out the front door onto the street and looked up and down. The way the man had spoken to her had annoyed him, and he just wanted to get a look at him. Taylor saw who he figured it would be walking up the street, meeting up with a group of young men, all around eighteen or nineteen years old. At a guess, Taylor thought that the man and woman had been dating, but it had finished, and he wasn't too happy about it.
Taylor went back inside. He didn't like bullies, and there was a time when his moral compass would have told him to go after him and threaten him to stay away or else. But that was a long time ago; he kept out of other people's affairs now.
At his table were the two drinks, and while he sat and waited, he smelt both drinks, and then he diluted the apple juice further; while he did so, the couple left, giggling into the night.
When the waitress brought his food, he noticed she had put her name tag on.

"Here you go," she beamed as she placed the food down.
"Thank you, Justine."
She paused, then she realised she had her name tag on, and she smiled brightly, but her eyes portrayed sadness, and before he knew it, he asked if she was ok.
"Oh, yes, absolutely." Justine smiled back, "enjoy."
Then she turned on her heels and walked back behind the counter.
Taylor ate his food; it was better than he expected, and drank his drinks. Then he paid, thanked Justine, and left. The man was still nursing his coffee at the table he was sitting at, watching his phone screen. It was late now, and while The Star Palace Café promised to be *open twenty-four hours for all your eating and drinking needs*, Taylor was pretty sure it could close soon, and nobody would feel that their food or drink needs weren't being met. He walked back to the flats and entered the main door. As he walked past the ground flats to the stairs, he heard shouting coming from inside one of them.
There are a lot of angry people around here, Taylor decided.
Once back in Flat 5, he undressed and showered, although he didn't feel much cleaner afterwards. He brushed his teeth, used the toilet and then, reluctantly, climbed into the bed. Taylor had been trained to sleep whenever possible when on assignment as you would never know when you may get the opportunity to do so again. So, despite the bed, despite the mould, despite the shouting and arguing from the other tenants,

despite all the additional noises outside, and despite the smell of old, musty stuff mixed with the damp, Taylor quickly fell into a deep sleep, having set his internal body clock to wake him just before dawn.

24

Taylor awoke just before the dawn broke on the horizon. The internal body clock had been taught to him a long time ago, along with many other things that he now relied on as second nature. He rose, checked to make sure he hadn't missed anything during the night and if Edgar had sent anything.
Nothing.
He used the bathroom, showered, and dressed in brown cargo trousers, a grey long-sleeved t-shirt and a grey zip-up hooded jumper. Today was going to be busy and mostly spent outside, and he didn't want to get cold.
He unlocked his phone, and once the secure padlock appeared, he called Edgar.
"Good morning, sunshine," was Edgar's opening statement. Edgar always seemed to be chipper and upbeat, no matter what. It was refreshing, not that Taylor would ever admit that to him.
"What do you have for me?" Taylor asked.
"I have been monitoring all night, lots of caffeine," Edgar elongated the word 'lots', indicating he had had many, then he paused and continued. "Anyway, I have analysed the guard patterns and how they rotate. The good news is, there is actually only a couple outside. Inside seems empty apart from some cameras in the main hall and the main open spaces. More good news for your morning is there are no cameras in any

bedroom or bathroom. This should be a nice easy walk in the park."

"You want to come and do it?" Taylor offered.

"I meant a walk in the park for you, a man of your many talents and…" Edgar trailed off, "…stuff."

"Thanks. How are they armed?"

"Machine guns. Can't tell you the make or model from what I can see."

"Only two of them?"

"Yep, from what I can see anyway."

"Great. Make sure I have all the addresses and keep an eye on it all. I'm looking for the house to be the most likely entry point. Scare him at home, and he won't feel safe anywhere then. However, I will be out all day observing the office, and I want to check out the other units you mentioned."

"Will do."

"Thank you. Let me know if anything changes."

"Sure."

"Oh, before you go, Edgar,"

"Yes?"

"Look into his love life. I want to know if he has a sweetheart, a wife, a mistress, a husband, an underage lover, anything that I may be able to use to pressure him."

"Gotcha."

Taylor hung up. It was going to be a dull day. But these days were necessary. They were the structure of any job, and he wanted to make sure he had the best chances of success. With Edgar keeping digital watch on the house and office, he decided to start with the unlikeliest place, if for no other reason than to rule it out. Taylor grabbed his surveillance equipment and left the flat, went downstairs; all the shouting had stopped for now. It seemed everyone was all shouted out and decided to go to sleep. He put the equipment in the boot, then he climbed in and started the engine. The air was still damp with morning dew, and the early morning silence was shattered by the roar of the Jaguar's exhausts. As if it was announcing to the world that the sun was coming, and a new day had arrived. Taylor hoped it woke the people who had been shouting, it was petty, and he knew it, but it still made him smile.

He entered the address of the unit and set off to begin his day.

The unit was on an industrial estate, a twenty-minute drive away and was the first of Maxwell Carson's properties from the flat, so it made even more sense to check it out.

It looked like an apocalypse film, or just a straight apocalypse had happened. The unit in question was big but dilapidated. It looked like part of the wall was crumbling, there were holes in the roof, and the windows were cracked and smashed. Taylor parked the Jaguar and got out. He looked around; all the buildings were the same. He felt he could scream, and no one would hear him. It looked like this whole place had just been deserted.

Why would Carson have a building here? He thought to himself.

Why would anyone? It looks like the whole business park was scheduled to be destroyed, but it got forgotten about and just left. This made no sense. Although it did explain why there were no images of Carson ever being here, why would he come here?

Taylor suspected he didn't even realise he still had his name buried deep down on ownership. He probably just forgot as he moved to better premises.

He walked up to the door; it was padlocked – with a fresh-looking one. All the joints and other locks were rusted, but this was shiny. Maybe only a few months old.

Was someone using it without Carson knowing?

Maybe.

Taylor moved around until he found a window he could scale. He climbed up, being careful not to cut himself and then dropped into the building.

It was abandoned, as expected. Most of the floor was open space with stairs leading to a mezzanine floor that looked to house offices. The area looked like images he had seen of car production lines; it was long and was supported by structure columns at intervals all the way down. Taylor walked slowly, scared of disturbing the silence. No one was here, so no one would hear, but caution seemed to tell him to play it safe.

He could see chains hanging from the ceiling about halfway down, no longer connected to whatever they used to support. There were old food wrappers with maggots and rats enjoying what was left lying around in a corner.

So, someone had been here. A squatter, maybe? Maybe he put the new lock on?
There was one room at the far end with a staircase bolted to the side for second-floor access. Taylor carefully looked inside – an old office. No computer remained, but there was a desk, and an old chair was in the corner. A whiteboard sat on the back wall. Probably many a meeting took place here. But nothing to make Taylor think it would draw any attention to cause Carson to come here. He made his way up the stairs, a simple metal staircase that creaked as he climbed and wobbled slightly. The second floor was much the same. A couple of offices were separated with a central walkway that led to an end office with a window that you could see out over the warehouse. He did a quick search of the offices and found them all the same as the one below. Nothing useful. Just office furniture. Nothing to suggest what it was used for and nothing with any names or details on.
Taylor walked back across the floor toward the window he had gained entry from. It was too high off the floor to be able just to climb back up as the floor sloped slightly. So he found a box he could stand on, but as he picked it up, Taylor noticed what seemed to be dried blood on the floor. Just a spattering. He followed the trail to a dark corner and found what looked like its origin. A dried deep crimson patch that looked like dried blood.
It looked like there had been a fight here. Someone had died here. Maybe the homeless man who squats here wasn't the first? Maybe he took it from someone,

killing him in the process. Maybe that's why it was better secured?

But where would a homeless man get a padlock?

It didn't matter. This place wouldn't be able to help him get closer to Carson. Taylor couldn't think of any reason why Carson would come here.

He used the box and climbed back through the window.

As he walked back to the car, he thought about what he had seen.

That building was useless. The only way that unit would be helpful to anyone, the only way it would get Maxwell Carson's attention, is if it blew up.

Taylor programmed the next address into the Jaguars sat nav and pulled out of the industrial estate, leaving it in his rear-view mirror.

He arrived at the office building. This was what he was expecting. It was a grand building; Tall, commanding presence and respect from the buildings around it. It was glass-fronted and must be thirty stories tall, maybe more. Probably more.

There was lots of glass and at the top, a huge sign stating it was:

Geologica Industries

Taylor parked in a public car park a few streets away, put his cap on, pulled up his hood and walked.

He entered through the rotating main door, entering the lobby. It was majestic. There were high ceilings with chandeliers, a waiting area that was bigger than some houses with several large sofas and a TV showing a promotional video about Geologica, saying how they were:

...working to save the world with their research into the water below the earth and solar power, and soon, fossil fuels will be a complete thing of the past.

There was a large reception desk, a metal detector, and a security door that you need to pass through before getting any further. Taylor could see the lifts behind the security point, on the left-hand side towards the back.

There were some desks further down with people working on them, but Taylor couldn't see what they were doing from where he was.

Everyone was dressed well, and the building was well presented. Anyone who entered here would definitely be convinced to donate, or sign up, or whatever they wanted you to do.

He moved around, trying to look inconspicuous, keeping his head angled away from the cameras that overlooked the door and the security station.

The receptionist saw him,

"Can I help you?" She asked politely.

Taylor considered just leaving, but then an idea came to him. Maybe it was easier to get up than he thought. He walked up to the desk, keeping his head low enough not to get caught but high enough not to look rude.

“Yeah, hi there, I’m supposed to be meeting my friend here, I’m not local, and we were going to surprise my sister; I haven’t seen her in almost a year. She works here, but it seems he is running late.”
Then Taylor pretended his phone vibrated and turned the volume off; he didn’t want to get caught out. He pretended to read a message.
“Oh, damn,” he said, “He’s stuck at work and can’t make it.”
He paused, allowing the receptionist, Tina, according to her name tag, to feel sorry for him before he pressed, “What floor is accounting on? I’ll just surprise her myself; she’ll be so excited.”
“Twenty-two, but unfortunately, you can’t just go up there. This is a place of business.”
“Please, I won’t be long, please it would make my day, and hers. I’ll just go up, say hi, give her a quick hug, and then I’ll tell her that I’ll see her later. I’ll be ten minutes. Tops.”
She didn’t say anything, but she was considering it.
“Ok.” She said eventually. “But you’ll need to pass through security.”
“Thank you, thank you so much!” Taylor put as much happiness in his voice as he could muster, and then he moved over to the security station.
It was easy to pass through. He had no weapons on him; this was recon, after all. He knew he would just scare Carson with his hands if he needed to.
Once through the scanner and the pat-down, passing both with no issues, Taylor went to the lifts. He walked purposeful but slow, taking in as much of the

environment as possible, how the desks were laid out, where the offices were. The whole area had the same white walls with emerald green detailing.

It was nice; Taylor had to give that to Carson. Whatever the reason he was going to sell, it wasn't because he had no taste.

He pressed the button and called the elevator. He felt exposed at that moment as all he could do was wait. He didn't like this feeling. Eventually, the lift arrived with a small ding as the doors opened. There were two men in suits standing inside, and after they had vacated, he went inside and looked at the panel.

There were thirty-seven floors.

Ok, in for a penny, in for a pound, Taylor thought and pressed thirty-seven.

Nothing.

He pressed again and noticed a little red button flash as he did so. A small keyhole was next to it. So, a key was required to gain access. He pressed thirty-six. The doors closed.

Taylor had made it further than he had imagined he would. He knew the sister act was a fifty-fifty chance, and thankfully it had paid off. There was no way the receptionist would know the name of every person in that building, let alone all their relatives. He hadn't given a name, so really, there was little she could do in ways of checking. Every company had an accounts department. It was a guaranteed department that he knew she wouldn't say they didn't have. So, a relative in an extensive department that was guaranteed, add in a little bit of play-acting and here he was.

The lift dinged, announcing the thirty-sixth floor.
Maybe there was a stairway that would lead up.
Taylor glanced out the lift and checked it was clear. It was, so he stepped out onto the landing.
This floor was just offices with closed doors. White walls, wood effect doors with small windows in and blue carpet. It was easy not to be seen here. He walked around until he found the stairs, went into the stairwell, in here was grey exposed walls, exposed metal steps. Any visitors to Geologica would be guided to the lift. It seemed the stairs were barely used. However, there was a stairway up. So, the stairs led to thirty-seven. There was hope yet. Maybe the office would actually be a better way of getting to Carson. He had expected more security. Taylor kept his face away from the camera and moved upstairs. Hopefully, he wasn't seen, and no one would come looking for him. He reached thirty-seven. It was locked. It required a key, code, a fingerprint, and a retinal scan to be accessed.
Damn it.
Locks could be picked, codes could be hacked, but the fingerprint and retinal would take too long, and that's if they could be broken at all.
This was a dead end.
Taylor heard a door open and close below him. Maybe he had been seen. Time to go. He went back down the stairs and could hear someone a few floors below

coming up. He re-entered thirty-six and moved to the lift. He pressed the button and held his breath.
Come on…
Come on…
Hurry up…
Taylor heard the stairwell door open, and a man spoke, telling someone else he would check and report back.
Damn it.
Taylor turned around, looked fast yet efficiently at his surroundings. He could hear the man open office doors, asking if anyone had seen a guy walking around.
Taylor was out of view of the cameras, and he needed to stay that way. There was an office at the end with no nameplate on the door. Either someone had just moved in and didn't have a name yet, or it was vacant.
The voice was coming closer.
He had to risk it. He moved, being careful not to run and draw attention to himself. He tested the handle, it opened. He went inside. The office was empty other than a desk and a cupboard for filing. He opened the cupboard door a touch, hoping it would be enough.
Then he looked through the drawers and found a stapler that would work. He hid behind the door.
He waited.
He could hear the man making his way around, asking anyone if they had seen anything.
He heard the ding of the arriving lift. *Too late now.*
He waited; he steadied his mind, preparing himself.
He waited.
Then the man opened a door that felt close, he asked his question, and he was answered with a yes, they had

seen someone walking past, going to Richard's old office.
Taylor realised he must be standing in Richard's old office.
Sure enough, the footsteps changed. They were no longer evenly paced and normally weighted; now, they softened. The man was no longer asking anything, he was coming closer, and he was ready.
But so was Taylor.
The door opened slightly; the barrel of a gun appeared past the window.
Why did they have guns?
What were they doing here that needed this security?
The gun retracted; the door closed.
Plan B. The man had missed the open cupboard door. Taylor threw the stapler, so it landed just outside the cupboard door. The office door opened again, the gun barrel passed by again, but a body followed it this time – the body of a man wearing a grey security uniform and a cap. The man slowly entered the room with his gun trained on the partially opened cupboard door.
He didn't check behind the main door as he entered; he would have seen Taylor if he had. But he didn't.
The security guard had just lost.

25

Once the guard was far enough into the room, the door began to automatically slowly close behind him. It was at this point that Taylor silently stepped up behind him. He allowed himself to be lost in the moment, listening for anything that would give him away, anticipating if the guard felt his movement and turned. Nothing came to him, his body telling him to proceed. Taylor reached around, knocked the gun out of his hands and grabbed the guard in a choke hold. He had to make sure the weapon was out of his grip, so there was no risk of it being fired. It was unlikely he could shoot Taylor at that angle, but any form of shot would raise the alarm. Taylor applied pressure, cutting off oxygen to the brain. The guard was tapping his arm and trying to reach around to grab him, to hit him, to do anything to get him to release his grip so his brain could breathe again. The guard passed out.

Taylor had no desire to kill a man he didn't need to. He was now under pressure. He knew he had a while before the guard would wake up, but he needed to make sure he had as much time as possible.

And he still needed to get out.

Taylor looked around the office, through the desk again, in the cupboards and the drawers, finding some black bin bags, and he decided what to do.

He stripped the guard down to his underwear, undressed and redressed in the guard's uniform. He put his clothes in the bag and screwed it up as small as it would go. Then Taylor used another bag to tie the guard's hand behind his back tight. It wouldn't hold long against strong force but would be enough to confuse him for a few seconds after he came around. Then Taylor put him in the cupboard, slumped on the floor. He closed the door, grabbed the open-backed office chair, and placed it over the handles, effectively locking him in.

He placed the gun and the radio, which he had turned off, in the desk drawer. He readied himself, and then Taylor left the office, making sure the door was closed behind him.

He kept his head down and hoped the cap would hide his face. The guard had been bigger than he was, and the uniform was a bit too big; it looked baggy.

In his mind's eye, Taylor looked like a kid wearing his dad's clothes.

It didn't matter. All he had to do was get out, and he could change again.

Would a guard use the lifts? Were they allowed to? Making them run up and down over thirty flights of stairs seemed improbable.

He took a risk, once again pushing the call button for the lift.

Mercifully, it arrived swiftly, and he entered, pushed for the ground floor, and made his way down.

The soft lift music seemed at odds with the fast, mental pace Taylor was currently using. He knew he could get out of this; this was in control. He was calm, but at the

same time, a thousand scenarios were running through his head.
Taylor had plans for if the lift stopped and he was trapped.
If the lift opened and there were guards with guns waiting for him and if security stopped him, among others.
The lift dinged – ground floor. The doors opened, but no guards were standing there with their guns trained on him. Taylor looked left, deeper into the building and saw the restroom sign he had seen on the way up. He walked over, calmly, in control, entered the restrooms and went into a cubicle. The restroom was white-tiled, and each cubicle was similar in size to most designed for disabled occupants he had seen.
Taylor changed back into his clothes and put the guard's clothes in the bag, making sure to leave the belt, badges, and anything else that would set off the metal detector in the bin. Then he left the restroom, walked across the lobby, and back through the metal detector. The guard didn't even ask to check the bag. Security was always more worried about what was going into a space than what was coming out of it.
Taylor smiled a thank you to the receptionist as he left. He walked back to his car and put the bag full of the guard's clothes on his passenger seat. Then Taylor put the address of Maxwell Carson's house into the navigation and drove away, wondering how long it would take for the guard to come around and to raise the alarm. He would, of course, be long gone, but he needed to let The Company know.

He called Edgar from the car and told him what had happened. His usual excitable self, Edgar thought it was awesome and wanted more details than Taylor wanted to share.

Reluctantly, after not getting the gossip he desired, Edgar agreed to report to the Administrator, and they would keep an eye on any reports. He said he would try and hack into the security and remove anything that may lead anyone to them.

Once this was done, Taylor returned to business.

"Do you have anything new for me?"

"Not much," Edgar said, "the day shift is pretty much the same as the night, but they don't have a patrol pattern, and mostly they lounge around on the garden furniture. Unless Maxwell appears, then they jump up and look busy."

"How many?"

"Four today. Four or five seems to be the average for the day shift. Only a couple at night."

"Thanks, Ed,"

"No worries."

"Anything on pressure points?"

"To be honest, he seems to very rarely leave the house. He doesn't seem to have any hobbies other than occasionally using his back garden for golf, and as far as love interests go, it seems to be a revolving door of women who come and go. I don't see any long-term partners, or even recurring girls. I have been able to access his network, and I have seen things, man, things that are burned in my brain forever. It's disturbing."

"Ok, but anything we can use?"
"No, sorry. Carson doesn't have any interest in women other than for disposable pleasure. I honestly think if you threatened him using them, he wouldn't care. He'd just get another three or four."
"Ok, thanks. Hey, could you look into that unit I went to this morning a bit more? Something about it seems wrong to me. Also, see if you can uncover any more little secret places he has."
"Ok, sure."
"Thanks, Ed. I'm nearly at his house now, I'll see what I can see, but I think this will be short from what I have seen so far; it will be a house breach, probably tonight. I'll need you on overwatch for me, so if you need to sleep, do it once I have scouted out the house."
"No problem, I'll be all over it, my friend."
Taylor hung up.
He continued to drive, the hum of the engine rumbling around him. The drive was a bit longer to the house. Taylor made a point of checking traffic flow and how easy the roads were to navigate. He could then time from Carson's home to the flat and give himself a rough timeline of how long in the real world it would take. The roads generally being quieter at night meant it should be easier, but he liked worse case scenarios regarding time keeping.
Being late was one of the few things he truly hated.
Taylor arrived at the house; it stood alone, set back into a field. A tall, wide, gated entrance with a long gravel drive led up to the main house. It was a big house. There was a massive porch at the front, and it was tall

and wide for only two stories. It had huge solar panels on the roof, and grass surrounded the whole house other than the drive. Around the back was a conservatory that looked bigger than most houses. It led to a patio with an Artisan garden furniture set and a long back yard, leading to a fence. The garden looked like it was designed as a golf driving range, only three times as long, and some woods backed onto the fence. There was a wall surrounding the house, 'the compound' seemed a more appropriate name. The wall around the compound encircled the house and ran down until it met the tree line of the woods.

It was a low wall, mainly there as show and as a border that was a statement of how much better at life Maxwell Carson was doing than anyone who drove past.

The benefit to that was it was low enough to scale quickly. In the documents Taylor had read about the house, he knew the back fence was electrocuted, ruling it out as the primary entry point. It seemed going over the wall was the best way.

He drove past and followed the road as it rose up. He parked up and walked across higher up on the hill to a vantage point that he could see the compound from. Taylor had brought his rifle's scope from the car and used it as high-powered binoculars. He called Edgar, placed the phone on the grass next to him, and looked down the scope.

"Hit me," was Edgar's opening.

"Edgar, I'm at the house. It's huge. Do you have the layout of this place?"

"Yes, it's sent to you now."
"Ok, thanks, open it up and tell me where his bedroom and his office are."
"Ok," Edgar drew the word out as he typed. "So, they're pretty much the same place. It seems his bedroom is on the second floor, back of the house, and his office is next door to it. The first room on your left as you come up the main stairs."
"Any panic rooms or escape routes?" Taylor asked.
"Not that I can see." Edgar paused, "the closest thing I can see is there is a back staircase; this leads down the back of the house from his bedroom. Maybe an escape route, may just be a staircase that leads to the back of the house. Y'know, for all those times your house is so big, walking down the stairs at the front of the house, and then walking all the way through your house is just too much to deal with."
"Yeah, thanks, Ed."
"You're welcome."
Taylor put the scope down. He had been watching the guards amble pointlessly around. Curiously, they never went inside. So, either Carson didn't want them inside, or he had more inside to protect him. He picked up the phone, took it off the speaker.
"Have you seen anyone enter the house? More guards? Private security?"
"No."
"Ok." Taylor nodded slowly, thinking.
"Should there be? I mean, he is just a business owner. I wouldn't expect any security at his house, if I'm honest."

"That's what I was thinking. Either, you don't think you need security, so you don't have any. Or you think you need it, so you have loads."
"What's your plan?"
"I'm sticking to tonight. Nothing I have seen leads me to think otherwise. I'll do it while there are fewer guards. Get some rest, Ed. I'll need you on camera duty later."
"Ok. Talk soon… Oh! I forgot; Maxwell Carson is also the named owner of another unit in another industrial area. This one is smaller and looks like it still does something. I have him going there on rare occasions, but nothing in the last few months."
"Thanks, but I think this is still the best play."
"Ok."
"Get some rest, and thanks again, Ed."
Taylor hung up and put his phone away. He wanted to put a camera at the gate, and one at the rear entrance, but the security cameras made that hard to do, and he didn't want to play his 'Edgar on the camera card' too soon. He would need that for later. So instead, he just drove back to the hotel. As he followed the road up the hill, there was a small car park for campers and people who liked to go along the walking trails or have picnics in the woods. There was one car, a black BMW, parked in the corner. He paid it no attention.
Once Taylor arrived back at the flat, he knew he was entering the assignments endgame. By this time tomorrow, he would be back down south. Possibly back in his apartment, possibly still in on the debrief. He had to make sure he was ready. From his point of

view, there was little more he could do. So, he took a quick shower and slept. His internal body clock set to wake him up when needed.

26

The woman knew that sooner or later, the man would show up at the house. She had positioned herself out of sight but where she could still see what was happening. She knew where she would be if it were her that was getting a look at the place. It had been a long few hours, the boredom almost bringing her to tears. She was more a woman of action. She always hated the sneaking around part, the watching part. The waiting part.

She wanted to just go in the house now and deal with it herself. It would be a lot quicker. She could be on a plane back to the states in a few hours instead of in a tree line, on a hill, waiting to see if this man would ever show up.

She heard him before she saw him. The loud car cruising around the corner below her, she didn't register it at first, but it slowed as it reached the house and then sped up after it had passed.

It was him.

Finally.

Sure enough, a short time later, he appeared. Exactly where she thought he would be. Exactly where she would have been.

He placed something on the ground next to him, and he was looking through a scope of some sort. It was hard to see from where she was. However, she took her opportunity. She slipped back into the tree line, moved around his position until she found his car. A black SUV. She placed the tracker on the inside of the wheel arch. She expected he would make his move soon, and she would need to be there when he did. The whole point of this was to have distance, to keep hers, and by extension, the Chairman's hands clean of all this rolling around in the dirt stuff. Once the tracker had been activated and placed, she moved back to her position to watch.

She saw him put his scope down and pick whatever he had put down on the grass up, and he put it to his ear. She realised it was a phone. She took a couple of pictures of him, but the angle wasn't great; she couldn't get a good shot of his face. He spoke for a bit longer, then got up and, keeping low, he moved out of sight. She waited for a few more minutes. Then once she heard the car start up and pull away, she waited until its sounds faded into the distance. Only then did she return to her car.

She made a call.

"Activate the tracker and send it to my phone." Those were the only words she spoke before she hung up. Then she called a number in America.

It was answered on the third ring.

"Yes," The Chairman said.

"All on schedule. I am tracking the third party to ensure no errors occur during the transaction."

"Good."

"I believe it will happen sometime between the next twelve to forty-eight hours."

"I await his call."

He hung up. She sat there for a moment, then she too started her car and drove away.

The woman sat in front of the laptop that was open on her table. She was watching the little flashing tracking beacon she had planted on the SUV. It was stationary, in a car park next to an apartment block– a block of 'flats' as they called them - and hadn't moved in over an hour. She was beginning to think this was where he was based.
She circled twice around the address that she had written down. It may come in handy later.
She wasn't sure when he would make his move. It made sense to approach at night. Over the wall, infiltrate quiet and get out before Carson can even raise the alarm.
But men, in her experience, very rarely did what she considered sensible. They liked to think themselves better, and they often tried the riskier way, or the more dangerous route. They thought it made them better, more superior, more dominant. What it actually made them, was stupid.

She wouldn't be surprised if he tried to find a way to cut the power to the fence, then scale it and take out all the guards, just to show he was superior. Then go in, disable all the cameras, and then go to Carson's room. But, then again, he had proved more competent in the alley. He was waiting for the target to come out for a smoke over instigating a full-on bar fight.
Maybe he did have a brain.

It didn't matter. As long as this man got the job done, it was irrelevant to her what method he chose to do it.

She set the tracker to beep and notify her if it moved. Then she ran a bath, undressed, slipped into the bubbles, and felt herself begin to relax.

27

Taylor woke precisely when he had planned to, his body naturally feeling it was time to become active and waking him. It was dusk now, and the sun was setting fast. The temperature had begun to drop, and there was a chill in the air. He took a quick shower, used the toilet, and freshened up as best as he could in the bathroom. He then realised he had not eaten all day. He checked the cupboard, but there was nothing other than some crackers and some old boxes of opened biscuits. The fridge also offered him no solutions as it contained less than the cupboards did. He decided there was nothing for him to eat in the flat.

He dressed in a t-shirt, jeans, and boots. He put on his jacket and picked up his cap.

He had time to get something to eat before he had to work, as Taylor wanted it as dark as possible when he arrived, but he also knew that, unless unavoidable, getting straight up and needing to spring straight into action was to be avoided. It was always better to give your body a little time to warm up if it was possible. In this case, it was, and while his body was warming up, it would need sustenance.

He took a walk back to The Star Palace Café and walked in. Again, it was quiet with only a couple of tables housing occupants; it seemed the kind of place people kept their heads down and kept to themselves. He walked back up the counter, but no one was there.

Taylor waited a few minutes before he pinged the bell on the counter marked SERVICE. Still nothing. He moved down the counter so he could see the back door. It was open; maybe whoever was working tonight was having a smoke break. He waited a minute or so more, then decided that was enough.

He went out the front door and walked around to the back of the café. There was a small car park with large industrial bins in the corner. *The waste for the café,* he assumed, easy for the bin collection to pick up.

Standing next to the bin was a man and a woman. Taylor recognised the woman as Justine from the night before. Did she work all the nights? Or shifts, maybe. He recognised the man too, the man who had been talking to her the night before. The rude man.

"Excuse me," Taylor said as he approached. "Can I get something to eat?"

"Can't you see I'm talking here, mate?" The man said in an arrogant tone. He looked around Justine's age, but up close, Taylor thought he must have been a couple of years older. He was wearing baggy trousers that failed to cover his arse and a hooded top that was low over his shoulders so the t-shirt underneath could be seen above it. He had scruffy blonde hair that looked like it needed a trim and blue eyes, although it was dark, so he could not be sure exactly what colour they were. *If he tidied himself up* a bit, Taylor thought, *he would be an attractive young man.*

"I've got to go back," Justine said as she tried to move past him, but he put his hand out across her to block her path.

"I'm still talking," he said.
"Alex, please, I have to go back to work. They'll fire me if they find out," she pleaded.
Alex was about to speak, but Taylor cut in. "Alex, c'mon, let her go."
"What you say to me?" Alex said, turning to face Taylor fully. "You use my name? Did I say you could use my name?"
"Don't you remember? Do you have memory issues?"
Taylor knew as soon as he said it, he shouldn't have. The last thing he needed was a fight in this car park. *Another time*, he thought.
"You want some of me?" Alex said as he took a couple of steps forward, closing the gap.
"No, I want some food. We don't need to do this."
"You don't tell me what I don't do or do do," Alex replied, his arms raising and falling at his sides as he spoke. Taylor was sure he thought it made him look tough; it made him look like he was trying to fly. Badly.
"Please, Alex," Justine was now in-between them, "just leave it. I'll call you later. I promise. Please, please just go."
Alex looked at Taylor, and every inch of him wanted to stare this idiot down and see what he had. He had more important things to do tonight, so, reluctantly, he looked away. This was enough to make Alex feel he had won; he was the bigger man, so he turned his attention back to Justine.
"Whatever. But I see you around here again, old man, and I'll break your fingers and tear out your eyes. Got

it?" With this, Alex half turned, made a gun shape with his fingers and signified shooting Taylor, then he walked away.
"You ok?" Taylor asked.
"Fine," Justine said, annoyance in her voice. Had he just made things worse for her?
Justine walked past him back to the café, and Taylor noticed Alex get into an old silver hatchback. It started up with a noise that hurt his ears in the otherwise quiet of the night. He noticed it had an aftermarket exhaust, the size of a drainpipe hanging out the bottom. He took out his phone and took an image of the number plate, and as he drove off and under a streetlight, he saw it was a Honda Civic.
Taylor then walked back across the tarmac and around the front of the café and called Edgar.
"Good morning, my main man Red," was Edgar's greeting.
"Edgar, I need you to run a plate that I'm sending you. It's not a great pic, but I need the details of its owner."
"New lead on the contract?"
"Maybe." Taylor lied. "Maybe not; it's an old silver Honda Civic. The owners first name is Alex if that's any help?"
"Sounds like you already know enough."
"Just see what you can dig up."
"You got it."
Taylor hung up, sent over the image, and walked back inside. Justine was behind the counter. As he approached and now there was more light, albeit

artificial, he could see the starting bruise of a black eye and the cut on her cheek.
"What happened?" He asked.
"Nothing," she said, turning her head. "Now," plastering her smile back across her face, "What can I get ya?"
Taylor ordered the same as before, tonight though, he could see her pour his drinks as he sat at his table, the same table, as the night before. She brought the drinks over and placed them down.
"Here ya go, hun."
"Thanks." He lightly wrapped his hand around her wrist in a non-threatening way of saying it's ok and after a micro-second, he let go.
"What happened?" Taylor asked again. "That Alex guy?"
"It's nothing."
"It looks like something," he motioned to her eye.
"Honestly, it's ok. It's my fault, really, sometimes I make him mad. I shouldn't, we were going to break up a while ago, but he didn't want to. He doesn't want me working here either, and he doesn't like that other men talk to me. I'm his girl."
"That's not right."
"Oh, no, I tell him not to worry, that I'm just serving. It's ok." Justine assured.
"No, I mean it's not right he does that to you. Have you told anyone?"
"It's ok, really, it is. Alex loves me."
"You should get out, call the police. I've seen what can happen,"

"Oh, no, he wouldn't hurt me, not really."
Taylor looked at her eye and raised his eyebrow.
"Oh, this?" She said, moving her hand to cover it, "this was just an accident, it was my fault, but even so, he still said sorry. It was an accident… Your food's ready." She smiled and walked over to the counter.
When Justine returned, she placed the food down quickly, gave a shy smile, but didn't make eye contact, and then she promptly left before he could say anything.
He smelled both his drinks, tested each with the tip of his tongue, then poured the water into the juice. He had seen her pour it, and it was doubtful Justine would have put anything extra in it, but old habits die hard. Taylor diluted the apple juice and took a sip.
He ate and drank, and when he was done, he paid. As he gave her the cash, he said, "call the cops, call someone to help."
She just smiled, said thank you and went back to the kitchen.
He left and was walking back to the flat when his phone rang. It was Edgar.
"So," he said as Taylor picked up, "done some digging on that plate, terrible pic BTW, but I was able to clean it up enough to get a number, and it belongs to one Alex Croft. Would you like more details?" He said the last part emulating the director's voice from the third floor.
Taylor didn't say anything.
"Ok," Edgar continued, "So, Alex Croft is a twenty-one-year-old man with an address about ten minutes

from where you are. I'll send it over now." His phone pinged with a *New Message* notification. "He has a record, fighting, property damage… says here, he put a man in the hospital, broke his jaw. Wow, really nice guy. He has also been to hospital a few times with his girlfriend, a one Justine, who seems to have been admitted with a broken arm, dislocated jaw, cracked ribs, broken collar bone and a broken foot, of all things. I can't see any relation or link between him and Carson, though. But I'll keep looking."

"Don't worry about it." Taylor said, "It doesn't matter, just archive it."

"Ok, sure thing."

"I'll call when I'm ready."

"I'm counting the seconds' mon amie."

Taylor hung up. Once back at the flat, he changed into one of his suits, selected his gun, a Glock 34, and his knife that he attached to his belt and prepared to go to work.

He hadn't planned on taking much; it wouldn't be a high combat assignment, so to bring a lot of weapons was overkill. He didn't plan to fire a single shot. He put on his suit jacket and holstered his Glock in the holder under his arm. He turned on the TV - raised the volume enough to be heard but not loud enough to disrupt others so they would come around and knock, asking him to turn it down - and left the remote on top. Taylor left the flat, walked down the stairs, down the hallway - the man in the ground floor flat was shouting again - out the door and got into the Jaguar.

The sun was completely gone now; the night was clouded over, blocking the attempts from stars to give some form of beauty to the blanket of black that lay across the sky.
It started to rain lightly.
He set off and started driving.

28

Although the woman had her eyes closed and was deep breathing, she wouldn't have called it sleeping. She would have said she was meditating.

After her bath, she had laid on the bed and let herself fall into a relaxed, almost tranced state of being. She was relaxed, calm, and yet alert at the same time. Every sense in her body was on, and she was aware of all the noises from the traffic and the people outside. She could smell the air freshener and the hissing sound it made as it activated and sprayed into the air. It sounded like it was right next to her, not in a completely different room. She was focused - hyper-focused- on what was happening around her.

She was waiting.

Her laptop made a noise signalling that there was activity. She was instantly alert. She was up and at the laptop, her towel still wrapped around her, and watched the screen. It showed the dot moving. It looked like it was time. *Was he doing it now? Or was he just out for a drive, maybe some night intelligence gathering?*

She didn't need to do anything, not yet. This was what they had hired him to do. It was his job.

She moved to the window and looked out at the sky; it was clouded over. It looked uninviting out there. Other house lights and business lights were on, but nothing looked like it wanted you to go out, brave the dark and enjoy life. It was dark, dank and horrible.

She couldn't wait to get home.
It started lightly raining. Tiny drops appeared and ran down the glass, almost racing each other to see which would reach the bottom first. She looked out.
Rain.
She hated England.
She went and got back on the bed and laid down. She took a few deep breaths and eventually put herself back into her meditative state and waited.

29

It was a shame that it had come to this. The man with the brown eyes had liked Officer Roberts. He had only used him on a few occasions, but he knew that was over now.

He knew it always came to an end, and usually, in similar ways, it was the business. It was how things had to go. The man with the brown eyes was a low-level guy, but he took pride in his work, and he believed, one day, he would get his recognition. His promotion. They would give him more to do, and he could prove he was an asset that they could, and should, trust.

But for right now, tonight, he was standing in Officer Roberts' garage. Next to the body of Officer Roberts as it swung slightly from its own weight, he was pretty much done here.

The body was hanging from the roof. It looked like a real-life game of hangman that someone had failed to guess and had lost the game. In a way, Officer Roberts had lost a game, but he had no chance of winning with his hand, and this was the outcome. He was still in his uniform.

It had been staged perfectly. Often when replicating a hanging, the rope marks are in the wrong place, or things don't line up, simple things that give it away.

Not this time. It was perfect. Right down to the angle of the rope on his neck and the kicked over box he would have stood on.
His badge and some personal belongings, a photo of his family, and a trinket his mother had left him after she had passed sat on a work bench at the top of the garage, next to his suicide note. Well, he hadn't written it, but it was a note saying he had committed suicide. It went into details about how he felt he had been responsible for the man's death in the prison cell and how he couldn't take the guilt of it all. How he felt he should have saved him, even though there was nothing he could do and what the investigation into him would do to him. He was responsible, and he had let everyone down. He didn't want it following him around, tarnishing his and his family's name. He said he was sorry.
It would be convincing enough. There would be no trace of what had actually killed Benjamin Sandel, and with Officer Roberts taking his own life over the guilt of failing in his duties, there would be no way of anything being leaked or inadvertently revealed. It was the last loose end that needed tidying up.

The man with the brown eyes left the house via the back garden, making sure not to be seen. Once he was far enough away that if anyone checked any phone calls from the area, it wouldn't show up, he made a call.
"It's done." He said once it had been answered.
"Well done," was the reply. "We'll be in touch."

The man on the other end hung up.

Mrs Roberts, Officer Roberts' wife of seventeen years, would come home from bingo tonight and find her husband's body hanging, find the note, and call the police.
They would not make it to eighteen years.
She was no longer his wife.
She was now his widow.

30

Taylor took a different route to Carson's house as he didn't want to drive past the front again. It was dark now, and he didn't want to make any unnecessary noises and put any of the guards on alert. He parked where he had before, far enough away but close enough that it wouldn't take long to get back once he was done.

He dialled Edgar.

"Go."

"Ed, how long can you block the cameras for?"

"As long as you want. I had a little peak earlier and recorded the loop, so I can just slice that in, and there will be no record of you being there. As long as you don't get caught, obviously."

"Obviously. Electronic security?"

"I can disable the alarm, but the doors are trickier and secure. Carson doesn't see his windows as a liability, though,"

"Ok," Taylor said, thinking.

"No hidden basements from what I can see."

"Great, when you loop the feed, I want everything you can take out, gone."

Taylor had been walking as he talked, and he was now near the wall, close enough to vault it quickly but still far away enough to not allow the cameras attached to it to see him.

The anticipation built inside him. He had a soft spot for this part, the build-up, the moment just before the moment. The hairs on the back of his neck were standing up, his brain pushing out anything that had no place being there while he worked, all his senses, his focus, aimed at this single goal.
"I see three guards tonight," Edgar informed him.
"Tell me when they are on the other side of the house."
"Will do. Your access point is the kitchen window, it's on the same side as you, and I see no electronic lock. It will be your best shot."
Taylor waited.
Waited to hear Edgar's voice.
Waited to be told it was time.
When the time was right, when the guards were on the other side of the house.

Edgar was halfway through saying 'Ok go' when Taylor shut the phone off and vaulted the wall.

The night was moist with the rain; this was good as it meant that the guards would be reluctant to go out unless they needed to. Real-life was rarely like the movies or video games, and guards didn't like walking around some guy's house on patrol in the rain any more than they liked doing anything else in the rain. The boss was in bed, so why not keep under cover as much as possible.
Taylor kept low, pacing across the grass to the side of the house. The window was a bit further down, but without Edgar on the phone, he was blind. Not for the

first time, he wished he had one of those earpieces he always saw on TV.
He crouched at the corner, his back pressed flush to the brickwork. He turned, so his front was facing it and peered around the corner, it was unlikely anyone would be there, but he was never one to assume.
It was clear.
Taylor made his move to the kitchen. The rain caused his clothes to feel heavier, to add resistance, but he kept going. He reached the window, lifted his head up enough to peer in. Lights were off, nobody moving.
He dislodged the window easily enough – for all his electronic security on the access points, the windows didn't even have a proper latch – foolish oversight.
Once inside, he pulled the window down enough that it was still easy to lift to get out again, but if a guard happened to walk past, he shouldn't spot it and think anything was wrong.
Taylor took out his silenced Glock. Intel had suggested that no one guarded the house at night. But intel, as he knew, could be wrong, so he was prepared. He moved silently toward the stairs. He had studied the layout and the documents provided for him, and he knew the layout by heart now. It would be easy enough, top of the stairs, second door on the left, his office was the first door.
He stalked across the floor into the main lobby; he was on the other side of the main entrance door now, as if he had just entered the house normally. There were giant stairs that boomeranged left and right and met in the middle at the top of the stairs.

It looks impressive, but why, Taylor thought, *would you need two staircases that basically started and finished together*?
He climbed the stairs; they seemed to be marble but didn't make too much noise underfoot. He was grateful he wore Converse as they removed the 'clack' of each footstep, but the rain from outside did cause them to squeak slightly. At the top of the stairs, he was met with a great corridor, and he was in the middle of it. He turned right and found the second door on the left. He put his ear to the door.
Taylor heard a noise.
Loud breathing, no, snoring. Carson was snoring. He tested the handle. Nothing. It was locked.
Damn it, he thought.
He looked back, went to the door for the office, tested the handle.
It opened.
He slowly pushed it open and entered. It was a grand room in itself. Bookcases lined the entire wall on the right side, they would have on the left too, but a gap housed a door.
There was a large oak desk in front of a large window that had a door to the balcony. There was an oversized chair in either corner of the room as you came in, facing the desk and standalone lamps next to each one.
Taylor made his way across the room to the door that would lead him to the bedroom. He decided to use this one; even if it were locked, he would use his lockpicks; there was more cover in here than the landing if a guard decided to brave coming inside.

Taylor tested the weight of the handle, brought his weapon close to his chest, and prepared…
He applied a small amount of pressure to the handle, it turned all the way down, and when he tested it, it didn't resist. It wasn't locked. He carefully pushed it open, leading him into Maxwell Carson's bedroom.
It was as he imagined it would be – a grand room for a grand man. There was a four-poster bed in the centre against the wall. The other door to the room was on the other side. There was a giant window that would have shown the large garden outback, only there were blinds drawn, and there was another door in this room that led to the balcony. There were nightstands made of thick oak next to each side of the bed, with a raised pattern on the ceiling that made it look 3-D, and the floor was wooden. There were large wardrobes, chests of drawers and cabinets against the wall.
There were two people in the bed. Taylor slowly made his way over, careful about his footwork. Walking on his toes, almost like a ballerina, a beautiful, delicate movement that portrayed near silence.
In the side of the bed closest to him was Maxwell Carson. He was a plump man with thinning hair. He was lying on his back, asleep, and his breathing was laboured. His snoring continued as Taylor made his way around the bed. In the other side was a woman; she looked tall and slender, her dress, shoes and underwear were folded neatly on a chair, her purse and phone were on the nightstand.

Her clothes were folded and placed neatly, her underwear on top of a deep blue dress. Her shoes were placed together, neatly under the chair.
This was not a scene of passion; this was a scene of professionalism. Before entering the bed, she had come in, undressed, and placed her clothes on the chair. The room smelt of the scent of sexual afterglow, sweat and cheap perfume. She had blue eye shadow on that looked like it was a close shade to the dress. Her hair, however, was an orange/copper shade that looked like box dye that had faded and grown out, as black roots were showing.
Taylor doubted this had been a scene of close, intimate lovemaking but more a case of a professional appeasing a client.
That was ok because if she had no attachment to him other than his wallet, she would be less likely to try and interrupt, or save him.
She, too, was lying on her back; she was a pretty woman. Taylor leaned over, placed his hand over her mouth and pointed his gun at her chest.
She opened her eyes, confused about what was happening, she saw him, her eyes wide with panic, but he put the gun to his mouth in a 'shh' gesture, and she nodded.
Taylor looked over his shoulder to the large wardrobe and gestured for her to get in it. She nodded. He motioned screaming as if playing charades with her, and then he held up his gun, so it was pointed at her face. He raised his eyebrows, and she nodded fast, panic causing her to over exaggerate the movement.

Keeping the gun trained, Taylor slowly removed his hand.
The woman didn't scream.
He moved back a pace.
She didn't scream.
She slowly slid out of bed, she was naked, and he could see needle and track marks on her arms. The limited amount of light that seeped in through the spaces in the window highlighted the glistening sweat on her body. She had a tattoo of an anchor on her hip, and as she padded over to the wardrobe, her naked feet pattering across the wooden floor, he could see one on her lower back as well. It was a heart, with a flower on either side.
It said 'live a beautiful life' underneath. Maybe that was the goal. Maybe she already was in her own way. She was not unattractive; in fact, her figure was pleasing to Taylor's eye. She had curves in all the places he liked a woman to have them, and he had to admit, if he saw her under different circumstances, he would have considered asking to buy her a drink.
She entered the wardrobe and closed it behind herself. Taylor picked her phone up and put it in his pocket. Then he turned his attention to the man making the noise. The reason he was here – the main event of the evening.
He paced around to Carson's side of the bed. He took his phone from the top of the nightstand, and he pocketed that too. He needed as much time as he could to get out afterwards, just in case. It would take Carson a lot longer to physically shout for help than call for it.

Then Taylor leaned over Maxwell Carson.
It was time.
As with the woman, he held his gun aimed at his chest, took a breath, and placed his hand over his mouth.
Maxwell Carson’s eyes burst into life, wide with panic.

31

Maxwell Carson lay there, his eyes wide, looking first down the barrel of the Glock 34 that was pointed at him, like a viper waiting to spit its venomous bullets at him and then up to the eyes of the man looming over him in the dark. He had light brown eyes, dark brown hair, and a full black suit with a deep red tie. Many thoughts raced through his mind.
Who was this man?
What did he want?
Why him?
How had he got in?
Where was his security?
As they fought in his mind to form an orderly line to try and become resolved, the man started talking.

Taylor moved the barrel up to his lips, once again using the motion for him to stay quiet.
"We need to have a little talk," Taylor whispered. "You are Maxwell Carson, owner of Geologica Industries. Correct?"
Maxwell Carson nodded. Taylor knew he was, but it was part of his routine to check and double-check as many things as possible when doing this type of assignment.
"You are in discussions about a buyout?"
Carson's face turned angry. He shook his head, and his eyes became emblazed with rage.

"No?"
Carson shook his head again.
"Ok, I'm going to take my hand away, you shout, or try to raise the alarm, I'll kill you. Understand?"
Carson nodded.
"Hands where I can see them."
He slowly took his hands out from under the sheet and laid them, palm up, on the duvet.
Taylor stood upright with his gun still trained on Carson.
The silence was almost deafening. It hung in the air, thick, like syrup over the interaction. Only a few noises from the woods were audible, and the slight breaks of moonlight caused lines of dim light to form across the entire room. Carson's face, with the pale light lines, looked like he was behind bars.
"I have it on good authority that you are in discussions about a buyout," Taylor said again.
"Well, you're wrong," Carson replied; his voice was low, just above a whisper. "An American committee came to me before, trying to buy me out. Offered me millions. But I said no. They are persistent; I'll give them that. They've tried many times since. But my company is just that. Mine. I'll be damned if I'm going to let some American pricks tell me what I'm going to do with it. But I'm assuming that's why you're here. To instigate a hostile takeover."
"Yes, they want you to sell, and I'm here to tell you that it would be in your best interest to. You have many years left in you, Mr Carson, and it would be a shame to have that future cut painfully short,"

Carson, still lying in his silk sheets, looked around the room, looked up again at the man dominating him and then down at the gun. Thinking.
"Ok. Ok, ok," he conceded, "fuck it. I'm rich enough as it is. I'll call them in the morning. I'll sell."
"Wise move, Mr Carson." He raised his gun slightly. "If I haven't heard by 8 am that you have called, I'll be back. You won't see, you won't hear me coming, and next time, I won't even do you the courtesy of waking you before I put a bullet in your head."
"Fine. Just fuck off."
"Have a good night, Mr Carson."
Taylor turned and left, back through thc office, down the stairs and, after checking it was clear, he climbed back through the window, moved across the grass and over the wall.
He crouched, waiting to hear if he was being followed, but when he heard nothing, he started making his way back to the Jaguar.
He called Edgar.
"Contract preliminarily fulfilled. He is calling in the morning. I have given him until 8 am. If not, I said I'd be back."
"Cool, I'll pass it on to the Administrator, and she will pass it on to the client."
"I'm going to stay another night in the flat, then once I have heard it has been done, I'll make my way back tomorrow and will be back at the studio for debriefing."
"Ok, then I guess I'll speak to you in the morning, mate."

Taylor hung up. He had now made the jog back and was approaching the Jaguar. He unlocked it, climbed in, removed his Glock from its holster and placed it on the passenger seat. He took a second to open the file he had been sent on Alex Croft. He had time left in the night, and it may be worth paying him a visit.
There was movement in the side mirror on the passenger side, Taylor looked over and reached for his gun, but suddenly there was a deafening smash, and glass showered him. He was punched, hard in the face and in his disorientation, Taylor heard the door open, and he was dragged out of the car, his gun, still on the passenger seat, out of reach.
He hit the floor and tried to gain recognition of what was happening. He could see sets of feet around him; he was being dragged, his suit and shirt had been pulled up under the friction, and his skin was being cut by the gravel and rough surface of the floor. He was dropped to the floor again behind the Jaguar. Taylor rolled over, looked up at the night sky. Two men stood over him. The noise still dazed him, the suddenness of the shattered window and the sensation of being pulled out and dragged, he half rolled, got one hand under himself to push him up, he couldn't think straight, but he knew he was in danger, he knew he had to position himself better.
He knew he had to fight.
At least he thought he would. But no sooner had this thought come to him, trying to get his body and his mind ready, had he heard a crack that rang out into the

night. He felt a blow strike him on the back of his head, and all thoughts left his mind.

As Taylor slumped to the ground, his head felt like it had been hit with a sledgehammer. Unconscious, darkness took him.

32

Maxwell Carson was not a man to be reckoned with. He had built his company on dirty money, and he helped supply some of the richest and most powerful men in the world. He was a man that people would think twice about before getting his coffee order wrong. He was responsible for helping some of the richest men do some of the worse things, and this American outfit had the audacity to think they could buy him out.

They had no idea what he was up to. They probably only wanted it for some of the rights he held to some of the sites. They weren't even a big deal. It was the stuff no one knew about that was what they would have been having wet dreams about if they knew it existed. When they couldn't buy him out, they sent this intimidator to scare him. This would not go without retaliation.

The sheer bloody nerve of it all.

The second the man had left, Carson had grabbed for his phone. It was missing; the bastard must have taken it with him.

He opened the nightstand drawer and grabbed the walkie-talkie inside, getting out of the bed, he pressed the send button,

"What the fuck am I paying you arseholes for?" He spat as he spoke, anger flowing through him.

"Boss?" was the reply.

“Some arsehole, fucking prick just tried to threaten me in my own fucking bed! Find him. Find him now!”
“Yes, boss!” an urgent and panicked tone came through. He heard movement outside as bodies sprang into action.
After a while, with Carson just pacing his room, the radio crackled.
“Found him, boss. He’ll be dead soon.”
“No!” He had other plans for this prick. “Take him out but keep him alive.”
A few moments passed.
“He’s out, boss.”
“Take him to the waste unit. I want to kill him myself. And get rid of his car.”
“Ok, boss.”

There was a noise across the room, and Carson turned his head sharply as the wardrobe door opened. A woman was cowering inside, peaking out.
“Maxy, is it ok?” She asked, her voice trembling.
Carson didn’t remember her name, and she had done nothing to warn him. She had also just heard he was about to kill a man. If somehow, she saw on the news or something that a man who looked like the one who had been here tonight was dead, she may get a crisis of conscience and try to turn on him.
“Yes, everything’s fine.” He reassured her in his calmest voice. “It’s ok to come out now”.
She did. She slowly climbed out of the wardrobe and started walking back across the room. She was hunched over and timid. She was naked, like he was,

and as he realised this, he wrapped himself in a dressing gown. She was sweating, shaking, and looked scared. She wasn't the best he had had, but she had done alright with his wants and achieving his needs. She had been ok for what he had paid. He had told her to stay the night so he could use her again in the morning, but that would no longer be happening. In the moonlight, as she looked now, he wasn't that bothered. She came to him. He kissed her, groped her, and she moaned a forced moan, pretending she liked it. He didn't care if she liked it or not. She wasn't here for her pleasure. He turned her around, and using the radio in his hand, he brought his fist down and hammered it into the back of her head, where the top of her spine met her skull.
She dropped like a dead weight.

Carson put the radio to his mouth again, "Come and get the slut; we're taking her with us."
"Yes, boss. On it."

Carson had no intention of selling. He just said what he needed to, to get that guy out so he could once again gain the upper hand. Once he had dealt with this guy, the prick who thought he could get away with pointing a gun at him, he would deal with the American problem.
They had no idea who he was.
"I'm fucking Maxwell Carson," he muttered to himself.

33

Taylor awoke suddenly. His brain had registered the water splashing his face and his instincts kicked in, and he was alert. He looked around. His head hurt; he could feel a lump and a nasty bruise on the back of his head. His vision was fuzzy, and he felt disorientated. He winced against the pain, and he tried to remember what his last memory had been.

Carson.

He was back in the car.

Something in the side mirror.

Noise.

Tumbling.

Dragging.

Two men.

That was it, that was all he could remember, but given how he now felt, he was sure he had been knocked out. He closed his eyes and tried to focus.

He was lying on his side on the floor, a hard, concrete floor and his hands were bound behind his back. Instinctively he tried to pull free. He couldn't.

He was cold. Very cold. He looked down at his body to find he was stripped and only wearing his black underwear.

The realisation started to seep in. He tried to look around. There were old concrete walls and a support pillar in the corner of his eye. In front of him was what seemed to be a large, metal container. It was round and

shallow, *but large enough,* he thought, *for someone to bathe in.*
On the other side, standing over everything was a figure, a plump, round figure of a man that his brain couldn't quite bring into focus.
Until he spoke.
"You fucking fucker!"
Maxwell Carson. Shit.
Carson started walking around the water-filled container.
"You piece of shit!" He kicked Taylor hard in the stomach. Pain bolted through him, and the air left his lungs. He groaned.
"You think, you think you can come into my house, MY HOUSE and point a gun at me!"
He kicked Taylor again.
Taylor had been ambushed at the car. He had taken Carson's phone, but somehow, he had got word to his guards fast enough, and they had found him; they had caught up to him.
"Here's the thing," Carson said as he squatted next to him, his voice now calm, controlled and deliberate. "I don't need anything from you. I know who sent you, and I will deal with the American shits soon, but you're mine for now. I don't need anything from you. I know it all. So, you're just here for my amusement."
He straightened up and kicked him again. Taylor groaned; his stomach and ribs felt like they were on fire. He spat onto the floor.
Hands gripped Taylor from behind and lifted him to his knees, his body protested, but it had no choice. Now on

his knees, Taylor could see inside the container. It was filled with water and ice cubes.
His heart sank, he knew what was coming.
Carson took a seat in what looked like an old office chair opposite him, the container of water separating them.
Taylor looked around, and he recognised where he was. It was the abandoned unit he had searched. The one that the homeless man had been living in. Only now he knew, there was no homeless man. Carson had put the fancy padlock on, and this was where he came to do things like this to people he didn't like. Taylor knew he could scream, but no one would hear him.
He tried to mentally prepare himself for what was to come and find a way for his mind to endure.
They say go to your happy place, but the reality was, he didn't have one. Didn't have any loved ones anymore. His family was gone, and he had no one he had any real feelings for in this world.
Taylor truly was, at his core, alone.

A hand grabbed his hair from behind and forced Taylor's face down into the water.
It was cold. Freezing. It felt like burning as it touched his skin. He held his breath as long as he could and forced his eyes to stay closed, but he couldn't hold it long enough and inhaled. As he tried to exhale, more water came in. He was going to drown. They were just going to drown him. He hoped, prayed that they wanted to torture him, it would give him time to think of something, a way out of this, but he was taking in

too much water. His lungs burned, and he felt this was it.

His head broke the surface of the water, pulled back by the hands that had kept it under, and he coughed, spluttered, and tried to clear his body of as much water as he could. As he drew air into his lungs, they pained against it.

He looked across at Carson. He hadn't moved. He just sat there, watching. A smile spread wide across his face.

Carson looked over Taylor at the man behind him that was holding his head.

"Again."

Once more, the water rose to meet his face as he tried to inhale enough air before he broke the surface. The water was freezing, though, and the moment his face was submerged, the shock caused Taylor's body to react, and he opened his mouth, screaming at the bottom of the container, air leaving his body in a trail of bubbles. Blocks of ice rested against his skin. They felt like red hot pokers in the cold of the water and the cold of the night against his body. Taylor thrashed his head, trying desperately to loosen the grip that held him under, but he couldn't. Between the angle and the pressure, the man killing him had all the advantages. Again, after what felt like an age, he felt his head resurface, and he spat, coughed, breathed deep, and tried to prepare for the next one.

Carson walked around and punched Taylor across his face, and he felt his lip cut and blood on his teeth. He spat out the blood that had pooled in his mouth.

Carson hit him, a left swing to the eye. It felt like a bat had hit him, and he would have been sent sprawling across the floor if the man behind him hadn't been holding him.
"Fucker" was all Carson said as he spat in his face, then told the man to put him under again.
Blood from his face mixed in with the water and started swirling around. Taylor tried to hold his breath again but couldn't for long enough, and again, freezing water entered his mouth.

The hardest part was that Carson didn't want anything; he asked no questions. Taylor wouldn't have given anything up easily; however, the opportunity to lie, to give a rest-bite from the water by talking, answering questions with false information, may have given him enough time to at least prepare for the next round of punishment.
As it was, no sooner had Taylor expelled the water from his lungs, he was submerged once again. His lungs burned inside him, the skin around his left eye was slowly getting ice burn as the punishment continued.
Again.
And again.
And again.
Over and over. Each time it was becoming harder to get air in before the next push under. His lungs burned fiercely as the ice-cold water was reluctantly forced into his system. Each time his body became weaker, putting up less resistance, he tried to keep his eyes

closed each time, but even that was becoming hard and eventually, after hours, but what felt like days, Taylor's body was too deteriorated to fight on. He couldn't take it.

In reality, it's hard to survive any form of torture. In films, you can always make a daring escape or get saved, and you're up and fighting. Taylor had tried to keep that mentality. Since before The Company, he had been trained to survive many forms of questioning and advanced interrogation -torture - techniques.

But there was no one coming to save him. The Company, as a rule, was a no-man left behind outfit, but he had reported in, and no one would suspect anything until Edgar tried to reach him after 8 am the following morning.

Taylor had no idea what time it was. He was too tired, too exhausted, to try and work it out. His body was broken. It was almost worse that Carson had just sat there, watching. Occasionally he would say something or make a comment, but his brain wouldn't absorb it, it would just sound like a muffled noise, and then he would walk around and give a punch or a kick in-between each one, but the reality was now Taylor was numb to it.

His whole body was numb; he was done. Much more of this, and he would just drown.

His head submerged again. The ice had been slowly melting, but it was still cold enough, and this time there was no struggle. He had nothing left. His eyes were open, and he looked blankly at the bottom of the

container. His thoughts eluded him, his brain no longer able to process anything. It was closing down.
This was it. His vision started to black as his head was lifted out again, and the hands let him go. Unable to support himself, he just fell, slumped to the floor in a heap.
Taylor's body was exhausted. His lungs were on fire, and he could feel the ice burn on his face above his left eye. It stung, but not as much as it had. His body had given up trying to register the pain it was in; there was too much for too long. He laid on the concrete floor, shivering, his muscles periodically spasmed involuntarily as they tried in vain to keep moving. Taylor could feel his heartbeat, and he knew he must still have one, but it was so faint, and he felt it wasn't long before it too, just gave up. He could see vague shapes of feet in front of him, he tried to turn his head to look up at the owner, but he was too weak. He heard a muffled voice, and his brain, as its last act of life, it seemed, strained his hearing so he could make out what was being said.
A voice, Carson's, saying, "I'm not done with you yet."
One foot rose up, and with his vision almost faded, Taylor watched it come back towards his face, barely registering it and completely unable to do anything about it.
Everything went black.

34

Eight am in England was three am in America. It didn't matter; people were working at all hours. The Chairman had fingers in many pies, so he couldn't be limited to just one time zone.

The woman had called and relayed that the third party had made contact and that there would be a call at eight am in English time from Carson to say that he would be selling.

The Chairman had told the group dealing with the sale that he was to be informed as soon as the call had been made.

Three am came and went. By three-thirty am, he had become impatient. He called the group for an update. Carson hadn't called.

Fine. Then Carson would be killed, and he would take Geologica from whoever was next in line. He called another number and arranged for them to find out how they would get access to Geologica Industries once the owner was dead and to put the necessary plans in place.

Then The Chairman made a call to a number in England.

A woman answered; it was nine o'clock in the morning by now.

"Yes," she answered hesitantly.

"No deal. No call." The Chairman stated, not even trying to hide the anger in his voice.

“Fuck.” The woman swore under her breath.
“Kill him.”
“And the third party?”
“They didn’t hold up their end. Cut off. Find Carson and put him in the ground.”
“Yes, sir.”
“We will talk when you return.”
She hesitated. “Yes, sir.”

35

The woman put her phone down. She had turned the tracker off once she had received word that the contract had been preliminarily completed as it had no longer been a factor. She had been awake and waiting for the hours to pass until eight am. Three am back home. Waiting.

Just before nine am, her phone rang. She had answered it on the first ring. The conversation had not gone well, and the Chairman had said he wanted to see her upon her return. She had to fix this. She would find the son of a bitch herself and make him call and do it there and then, with her gun to his head. Just like the guy should have.

She didn't know what he had done, only that he had failed.

She had recommended him. It came back on her. She needed to resolve this so when she got home, it wouldn't be the worst-case scenario.

She was stuck in this god forsaken country for a while longer.

She called The Company, withdrew the contract as it wasn't completed.

She then opened her laptop and brought up the GPS tracker number, and looked. It was off. No signal. Had the man found it?

Its last location was a field about half an hour away from its previous stop near Carson's house but had then died. Maybe he took it out there and destroyed it so she couldn't track him?
She would start at Carson's house. Then his place of work.

She got up, dressed in black jeans, a black turtleneck jumper and a brown leather jacket. She packed her things in the car and drove to the house. She parked where the SUV had parked before; she wasn't expecting the guy to be back yet. Maybe he would come back to finish the job? Perhaps not, but either way, he had failed, and it was up to her to finish it now. She looked into the compound. No movement. No guards. Nothing. She moved in for a closer look but still couldn't see anything. She jumped the wall, timing her movements to the camera rotations. She looked in a few windows, found nothing. No movement at all and couldn't get eyes on Carson.
She withdrew, keeping low and timing her retreat path. Once over the wall, she returned to her car. As she approached, her feet crunched on broken glass.
So, Carson had had all that excitement last night and then decided to go into the office this morning, had he? She started up the BMW and pulled off, heading towards the offices of Geologica Industries.

36

The Administrator was disappointed to hear that the client on the Maxwell Carson assignment had withdrawn the contract due to an unsatisfactory conclusion. She was disappointed and surprised by Agent Red. When he had reported to Edgar early that morning, he had seemed confident of the contract's swift resolution.
An investigation would be launched upon Agent Red's return to find out why. The Company did not take unsatisfied customers lightly, and she planned to get to the bottom of it.

She entered the room on the second floor of the tattoo studio and walked up to Edgar's station. He was sitting, looking at his screen. His curly hair bounced as he turned to face her.
"Agent Red is to report to me upon his arrival back, please." The Administrator instructed.
"Yes, ma'am." Edgar's usual chatty responses were kept concise for the Administrator; she was not very receptive to them.
"When is his ETA, please?" she asked.
"I don't know, ma'am."
"Does he know of the cancelled contract? If so, what's his reason?"

“I don’t know, ma’am. He hasn’t checked in this morning. Nor has he responded to any messages or attempts at contact.” Edgar replied.
“Where is he?”
“I don’t know. His phone is off, and I can’t track it.”
“When he checks in, tell him to come and report to me upon his return.”
“Yes, ma’am.”
The Administrator’s voice softened more so, and she lowered her tone. “Find him, Edgar, make sure he is safe. If we need to send a response team out to get him, tell me, and the nearest team will be dispatched.”
“Yes, ma’am, I will do ma’am.”
The Administrator left, and Edgar began searching, using everything he had access to, to find where Red had gone. He tapped into the house’s front cameras at Carson’s home, looked at the footage that would have been used if they hadn’t covered it. Nothing. Agent Red had been careful even when he hadn’t needed to be. He wasn’t showing anywhere. Edgar searched cameras around the roads, but they were few and far between and showed nothing.
He carried on searching, a niggle, a voice in the back of Edgar’s mind said he needed to find Red.

37

Carson was not at his office, or if he was, they told her he wasn't. The woman asked to use the bathroom, and she was allowed through; there was a quick light pat-down, but nothing near what she should have had. *Women are less dangerous to men.* She reminded herself. They very rarely see women as physical equals and, as such, continually under-estimate them.

She went to the bathroom, then snuck up the stairs. There was a lot. Thirty-seven flights of them before she reached the locked door. She didn't waste much time as the room was soundproofed, and she couldn't hear anything.

She went back down and left. She walked around to the car park; his car still wasn't in his reserved spot. Maybe he had a driver? She had never seen a vehicle at his house either. No car, of course, didn't mean he wasn't there, but it added to her doubts.

She left.

She was out of ideas.

The guy.

The guy may know; he had spent a day scouting out the locations. He had done more groundwork. The groundwork she would have done if it had been her doing the job. She could do it now, but it would save her a lot of time if she just got him to tell her.

She opened her laptop on the passenger seat, loaded up his routes from the tracker and loaded the address into the navigation.
First, she would try the flats he had parked outside of. If the man dropped the tracker, there was a good chance he was there, maybe planning his way to finish the job.
She began driving.

She arrived and parked around the corner. She wanted to keep out of view as much as possible. She walked around and into the block of flats. It was grimy and dirty and the last place anyone would think to look; it was the kind of place no one would want to stay. She walked quietly, carefully listening through the doors, assessing who was inside. Most places had noise. People talking, kids shouting and playing, some had TV's or radio's playing, entertaining the people that had the misfortune to live there. A couple had people having sex inside them.
She made her way to the top floor and back. Did the run a couple of times, listening. She found that two were consistently quiet. All the others had noise so were more likely to be occupied. She picked the lock of the first one, Flat 7, and entered. It was dark, dank, and smelled of must. She had a quick, quiet search, her knife in her hand ready, and she heard sleeping. Deep, rhythmic breathing. She followed it to the bedroom. A man was sleeping in the bed, but he wasn't the man she was looking for.

He stirred and saw her; a confused look spread across his face as he tried to determine who she was and why she was there.
“Who are…” he started saying before she raised her finger to her lips and shh’d him.
She entered the room, the hand holding her knife behind her back. She swayed her hips as she moved, exaggerating her hips and her figure. His eyes lit up. He looked like all his Christmases had come at once. He didn’t care why she was here anymore; he was just glad that she was.
She made her way to the bed, slipping the knife into the trouser band at the small of her back as she did so. She slowly unzipped her jacket, looking at him in the eye as she did so, holding his stare. His smile grew wider, and he had stained yellow teeth from too many years smoking.
She stood next to the bed, waved her finger to beckon him up to meet her. He started to rise; he was leaning on his elbow to push himself up, moving ever closer to her lips to kiss her. She whipped out the knife and embedded it into the side of his neck; as she did so, she put her left hand over his mouth and guided him back onto the bed, his eyes looking at her, confused, as the life drained from them and soon, they glazed over.
“Men.” She said as she turned. She cleaned her blade in his bathroom and left, closing the door behind her.
The other flat she needed to search was higher up. Flat 18. Again, she picked the lock and entered. The layout was almost identical, as she imagined all the apartments – flats – were, but this one was more

homely. Plants scattered about the place, bright colours and pictures drawn by, and photos of kids were dotted around. She scanned around and searched quickly but competently before confirming her initial thoughts.
This isn't the place.
She left, closed the door after her and made her way back to the BMW. Once inside, she thought about her next move.
She looked at the tracking line and decided to check out the last known spot.

She drove to the last known location on the map. It was a field in the middle of nowhere. She parked up a short way down the road in a lay-by and walked back. She was glad she wore boots as the field was muddy, but just as she was climbing over the gate, she spotted an access road running along the side leading to some large barns.
She climbed back down and walked around, careful to look casual, like she belonged there, but also alert that if the actual people that did belong there saw her, she could react.
She reached the barns up the uneven accessway. She opened the first one to find an old car sitting inside it, in the far corner. It was covered in dust, and the tyres were flat and looked as if it hadn't moved in years. She moved up to the next one, keeping low. Inside this one was three cars. Well, what she imagined had once been three cars. They were all burned out with very little to show what they used to be.

Two were small. Hatchbacks, she presumed. One was larger, an SUV. It looked like it was fresh and small amounts of heat were still rising from it, and the ground around it still sizzled with the last remaining embers.
A controlled fire.
Recently.
The woman wasn't a car person, but she thought she knew what she was looking at – the man's black SUV, or what was left of it.
Had he parked it there? Was this what he does? Were the other two also his that he had destroyed, covering his tracks?
Or had something else happened?

She left, running different scenarios over in her mind as she walked back. She had no leads left, no way of finding Carson first. She did know, however, sooner or later he would go home. She would just have to stake it out and be patient.
By the time she had delved herself into any other options and got traction, chances are he would be home anyway.
She began the drive back to Carson's house.

38

Edgar hadn't found Red, and he had no idea where he was. He tracked everything he could. He had told himself he would give it a few more hours, recheck everything, search more, harder, deeper, and if he still came up empty, he would report it in.

The forty-eight hours weren't up yet, and he knew the protocol was still in place. He was no longer on an active assignment, so the risk was low. He must be sleeping in or got caught up in doing something else. He hoped.

39

A spark ignited in his mind. His brain seemed as if to turn itself back on.

He wasn't dead.

Taylor started to stir. He could feel his head pounding, his chest in agony, his face hurt, his whole body, in fact, was reeling and still trying to assess what the hell had happened.

He reached up to his face; his hands were bound in front of him now.

Suddenly he was moving. Yanked up into the air by his wrists, his arms felt like they were going to be ripped from their sockets. He was now hanging, his feet clear of the floor. He was being suspended by his hands.

He looked up, his neck sore, and saw his wrists were attached to a chain that pivoted over a beam in the roof and came down next to him. He followed it with his eyes and was met by the sight of a man holding the chain, attaching it to the pillar he was hanging next to. The man wore a uniform, like the one from somewhere he had seen before.

Where had it been?

An office?

Geologica. That was it. He wore the same uniform and cap as the guard at Geologica and the ones at the house.

The house.

The house… Carson, Maxwell Carson's house. He must rotate guards.

Then more came back to him and Taylor realised the situation. The danger that he was in.

His body was weak, but he had some control over it. It ached, but it worked.

Ok, he started thinking fast.

I'm alive.

I've been tortured by ice water.

They hadn't killed me.

Why?

He could still get out of this.

Where was Carson?

Then Maxwell Carson came into view, walking around from behind him.

"You're awake," Carson grinned. "Good, for me. Bad, for you."

"What do you want?" Taylor asked. His voice sounded weak, barely more than a whisper, strained and soft. He barely recognised it himself.

"Me?" Carson placed his hands on his chest as he replied, then dropped them, scrunched his face in anger. "I want the man who threatened me! Who put a gun to my face! To die. Horribly. And slow."

Taylor said nothing in response; he didn't trust his voice.

Carson came up to him, a knife in his hand, and then he placed it above Taylor's left eyebrow, about halfway, and slowly dragged it in a crescent moon shape around the edge of his eyebrow to his temple. Taylor protested through gritted teeth, shouting at the pain but keeping his mouth closed so as not to give him the satisfaction of a scream. It just sounded like a loud groan. His whole body tensed.

"It's good you're back," Carson said as he took the blade away, looking at the blood on the tip. Taylor could feel the blood running down his face, onto his cheek and dripping onto his chest.

"While you were gone, I only had this one to play with." He put his hand on Taylor's chest and pushed so he swung around. In the corner was a woman who Taylor recognised – the woman from Carson's bed. She was lying on the floor; she was still naked but had been badly beaten and had been cut all over her body. Deep wounds had been lashed into her arms and legs, across her chest and her face was puffy and bruised, her lip was bleeding, and she too had a deep crescent moon cut from her eyebrow to her temple. From what he could see, she must have had at least fifty cuts, and that's just what he could see. He expected her back to be the same. Her cuts were deep, and she was slowly bleeding to death. She wasn't going to be alive much longer. She looked weak, her chest rose and fell to a shallow rhythm, and she had a look in her eye, a faraway look like she was already dead, and she was just waiting for her body to catch up.

Despite not knowing this woman, rage coursed through Taylor's body. He felt his blood pump, and anger replaced the pain in his system.

This man, Carson, was a monster, and he would die. He was going to get out and find a way to kill him.

Maybe, or maybe that was his reaction to keep himself fighting because he knew that the cut he had just given him was the first. He knew that he was going to end up the same. He was turned back to face the front and the woman, once again, was no longer visible.
"Were you in my office recently?" Carson asked.
Taylor said nothing.
"A man," Carson continued, "got into my office building, went to the top and started snooping around."
He was pacing in front of him, turning the blade handle in his right hand and touching the tip with his left index finger.
Taylor said nothing.
"Was it you?"
Nothing.
"This man, who looked like you, I must say, then attacked one of my security staff, stripped him and locked him in a cupboard. He was there for hours, the poor man."
Nothing.
Carson approached him, put the blade on his chest, just under his right collarbone, and slowly dragged it down while saying slowly, with venom in his words, "Was. It. You?" He stopped when he reached the nipple.
Taylor cried out through gritted teeth, trying to suppress what he could. He knew he wouldn't be able to take much of this before his body gave out. He was weak and still in pain from the water torture, and he knew how weak his body was.
His mind went back to the woman. She must have screamed; she must have cried out and begged him to

stop. But he hadn't. This man needed to be put down like a rabid animal. If he got the chance to do it, Taylor was going to take it.

"I don't need you to answer me, really," Carson was talking again, "I was just wondering. To be honest. I don't care, and if you were wondering, no, I didn't sell my company."

As he was talking, Taylor let his mind think that if Carson hadn't made the call, the Company would have tried to get back in touch with him. Or at least wondered why, after the deadline had passed that he hadn't checked in.

There was sunshine outside; it looked to be early afternoon. It shone in through the smashed windows and the broken ceiling. Would they come looking for him? Yes, of course, Edgar would be looking for him, and if he couldn't find him, then a react team, probably just another agent at first, would be sent to find him. He would track them here. Taylor would be saved.

He had to survive forty-eight hours after initial missed communication for that to happen, though.

Forty-eight hours. Could he do that?

He had been here a good few hours already, but he was broken and weak. How much longer did he have in him?

Taylor looked around for a way out. Saw the dried blood he had seen before, not a fight between homeless men, another person who had been brought here, been through this and then probably executed.

Was this how it ended?

Hanging here, in this old, abandoned unit, in this old abandoned industrial estate. Hanging from the ceiling or a bullet to the head.

This wouldn't have been his choice of ending.

Carson punched him hard in the fresh-cut, and Taylor swayed a little and tried to absorb the pain. It was getting harder and harder to do.

"I can see you like to take care of yourself, Mr who-ever-you-are. You have a nice body. Toned, muscular, but not over the top. I can appreciate that." Carson lightly ran the blade down his chest, down his stomach, down to the pubic bone, and then started to run it back up again. Then Carson stabbed it into him, pain shot to Taylor's brain, and he couldn't help it; he screamed out as the burning sensation tore through him. He took a breath and screamed again.

"That's better," Carson said as he laughed. "That's more like it." His phone rang.

"I have to go now, Mr who-ever-you-are. But my friend here is going to keep you company, and if you try anything, I've told him it's ok for him to kill you." Carson put the knife down, stepped away and answered the phone. Taylor could hear him as he walked; it seemed he was setting up a meeting at the den.

What was the den?

Where was it?

He hadn't come across anything like that when he had been scoping places out.

"It's just you 'n me now, pal." The guard said as he stepped into view, blocking Carson as he left, he heard the doors clang as they closed. If he could get out

before Carson came back, he could get help, and then he could come back and finish him off.
The guard punched him, Taylor groaned and swung, the guard hit him again.
"You're like my person'l punchin' bag ain't ya mate."
Taylor looked around at the room, not much to help him. The water container was still there, some broken glass on the floor, the old food containers next to the woman and the woman herself, but she was closer to death with every breath.
Damn it. The guard was his best hope.
"I ain't your pal," Taylor said, putting as much depth to his voice as he could. His lungs still burned, and his throat hurt. "And I ain't your mate. Prick."
This got a reaction. The guard squared up, twisted his face, "I'm gonna fuck you up, arsehole."
"It's a good thing I'm tied up. You may actually be able to do it." Taylor needed the guard angry, not thinking straight, off-balance and emotional.
"C'mon then, dickhead." Taylor breathed, trying to sound like he had more in him than he did. His voice was still weak, and every word was like razors in his throat, but he needed to keep going, keep pushing him. He could see it in the guard's face, he was getting more and more frustrated, angry and Taylor knew he would never let him down for a fair fight, but he didn't need him to; he just needed him closer, one more step.
It worked.
The guard came in closer. Now or never.
The second he was in distance, Taylor used as much energy as he could muster and slammed his forehead

into the guard's nose. The force rocked his head, made his headache worse and disorientated him. He knew head butting was a bad move, it was never as clean as it looked, but it was all he had available to him. There was a sound of bone-breaking, and Taylor knew he had just broken the guard's nose. The guard doubled over in pain, his hands coming up to his nose out of reaction. With the guard now bent over, Taylor was able to get his knee on his shoulder; he could only raise one as the stab wound meant trying anything with the other side would be excruciatingly painful and may cause him to pass out. He braced himself and prepared for what came next. The guard reacted, bucked up, and Taylor used the momentum to push himself up and, using all the energy he could, shouting with exacerbation and putting everything he had left into it as he knew he would only get one shot at this. He screamed as the muscles in his arms burned and twitched with exhaustion.

The rope slid over the hook.

He had done it!

With nothing supporting him now, he fell off the guard's shoulder and crashed to the floor. A new, fresh pain shot up his back, and he moaned, but he was off the hook.

He was free.

Almost.

The guard had recalibrated and was once again a threat, his nose had blood flowing from it, and the bruising was already showing itself. Taylors' hands were still bound by rope, but his legs were free. He scrambled

up, his body just wanting to give up and rest, but he forced it to work, adrenaline giving him the strength he needed to try and keep himself alive.
Taylor charged; he slammed into the guard with his shoulder and forced him back with whatever strength he could summon. Then he pulled away, and power kicked him, the sole of his foot hitting the guard's chest, putting him back a bit more, then before the guard could come back with anything, Taylor rammed his shoulder into him again and pushed him as hard as he could. He hit the edge of the water container and toppled in, his head and shoulders becoming submerged under the water.
The guard drew his head up, took a breath of air and started the climb back out, but Taylor was on him, forcing his hands, chest, and head back under. He was in the tub now, too, kneeling on the guard's shoulder joints and sitting on his chest. He put everything he had left into his arms and hands, pushing down on the throat to keep the guard underwater.
The guard scrambled in panic, scratching at Taylor's legs, trying to get himself free, he tried to lift his neck enough to break the water for air, but it was too deep. Taylor looked into his eyes, letting him know that he was going to die. No one was going to be lifting him out of the water so he could gasp at the air again.
After a time that felt like an age, the struggling became less and less, and then eventually it stopped altogether, and the last stream of air bubbles left the guard's mouth and rose to the surface. Taylor stayed where he was, partly so he couldn't be surprised if the guard

were playing dead, but mainly because he was exhausted and had nothing left. After a few more minutes, he pivoted himself over the edge and fell to the floor. The guard's legs still hung over the side, and Taylor lay on the floor, panting, trying to control his breathing, drawing air in, and just taking a moment to allow himself to feel alive. He couldn't have moved if he'd wanted to. He rolled onto his back and looked up at the roof. He could see spots of clouded over sky through the parts of the roof that were missing. He realised, lying there, naked bar his underwear, soaking wet on the dirty concrete floor on that old, abandoned unit, looking up at the overcast clouds passing over him, that he had never seen a more beautiful sky.
The sensation of still being alive, the wave of relief and joy that he had survived, washed over him. He couldn't help it. He laughed.

40

Once Taylor thought he had enough energy, he got to his knees and shuffled to the water container. There was a knife in a little leather holder on the guard's belt. He fumbled for it, his hands and fingers struggling to co-operate with his brain, but eventually, he got it out, opened it up and was able to cut through the ropes.
He pulled the guard out of the water and left him next to the container; he then tried to move over to the woman lying in the corner, but his legs were weak, and he stumbled. He made the last few paces on his knees. He looked down at her, into her eyes, and he knew she had gone. Her chest never rose, and she had no pulse. Taylor closed his eyes, and for a minute, he just sat next to her. His side was hurting, and he placed his hand across himself to put some pressure on it. There was still a trickle of blood leaking from the wound, and he needed to get it patched up. He looked at her body, looked at the wounds and damage that had been inflicted upon her and the way she had just been left to die in the corner, discarded like she was nothing. He was tired, achy and in pain, but right then, his biggest overwhelming feeling was anger.
He was an enemy combatant in Carson's eyes, he was fair game, and Taylor understood this, but this girl, she didn't deserve this. What had he done to the others who had been here? The dried blood on the floor, what else had been done here that he couldn't see traces of?

Taylor knew he had to go; it would only be a matter of time before Carson came back or called the guard lying on the floor whose phone was now destroyed from water damage and realised something was wrong. He went back over and dressed in the guard's clothes. He had no idea where his clothes were, but he couldn't see them or his stuff after a look around. Maybe they had left it all with his car.
He did, however, find some old dust sheets in a cupboard. They were covered in paint, the same shade as the walls in the ground floor office. They weren't the best, but they were the best he had. He used them to cover over the woman.

Taylor stumbled over to the door. Thankfully, it wasn't locked, and he went outside. The uniform fit him ok, but the top was soaked through and weighed him down, but they were better than walking around in just his underwear. It was overcast today and seemed to threaten rain later. He looked around for his car but couldn't see it anywhere.
They must have it somewhere else.
Damn it.

There was a car, though. It was a black Range Rover. Taylor tried the handle, it opened, *yes*. And the key was in the key space in the console. *Yes*. Things were starting to turn around.

Then a silver Range Rover appeared, it stopped, and Carson got out of the passenger side; he looked over at his guard standing by the car and looked confused. Taylor wanted with every fibre of his being to go over and crush his head, pound him into the dirt, but he was weak; his body was exhausted and hurt all over. He knew he needed to get medical help soon for his stab wound mainly, and everything else, if he was honest. Plus, if the driver had a gun, he would be dead before he got close. He needed to run.

Carson figured it out, though, pointed at him, shouted, and jumped back in the silver Range Rover.
"For fuck's sake," Taylor said to himself, heaved himself up, started the black Range Rover and floored it. The wheels kicked up loose surface dirt as the tyres gripped for traction. He weaved out through the access roads in-between the units, his arms ached, and the stab wound in his stomach sent pain through his body as he was sat and put pressure on it.
The silver car was right on his bumper. In the rear-view mirror, Taylor could see Carson shouting orders at the driver and pointing.
He threw the black car through the turns, and finally, Taylor broke out of the twisty, narrow roads and out onto the main streets, narrowly avoiding a car passing the entrance as he did so. The car screeched its horn at him, but he paid no attention. He just put his foot down and sped away.

41

The Range Rovers barrelled down the street, one after the other, weaving and dodging through traffic. It was a big car, and the narrow country roads were not wide enough to allow any mistake in the navigation of the wide vehicle. Ditches, high banks, and hedges lined either side, enclosing the road and only allowing one route.

Taylor was grateful it was a two-lane road as he straddled the middle, but each corner was blind and harsh, and if anyone came the other way, it would cause difficulties. The silver Range Rover, pursuing him relentlessly, bobbed in and out of view behind him as he rode the bumpy, uneven surface and briefly became lost from his rear-view mirror as he turned the corner, but only to appear all too soon again.

Taylor knew he needed medical attention, but he couldn't go to a hospital while being pursued, and he didn't have his phone, so he had no way of contacting The Company securely. Besides, he wanted to stay under The Companies radar for a while now while he dealt with the Carson situation his way. He did, however, have a destination in mind, someone local who could help him, albeit reluctantly, he imagined. All he had to do was lose his chaser and get his bearings.

He turned another blind corner, the high hedges caging him in, a car was coming the other way, a small estate

car that braked hard as the giant Range Rover came flying into its view. Taylor yanked the wheel and was able to avoid it. Just. The silver car avoided it too, managing to swerve at the last minute and then it piled on the speed to catch up again.
Taylor saw a sign for a main road at a junction up ahead, and he slammed his brakes on, trying to scrub enough speed to be able to make the turn. He reached the junction and turned the wheel; the car skidded, half made the turn, skidding across the central markings into the wrong lane. Thankfully, it was vacant, and as the tyres squealed and the body of the big car leaned, Taylor thought it would tip over. Mercifully, it stayed on all its wheels, and once it straightened up, he piloted back into the correct lane and accelerated.
He glanced back as the silver car turned into view, they had seen what he had done and been able to make the corner a lot smoother, and the time he had gained had vanished.
The Range Rover was an automatic, which he was glad of as it meant no time wasted fiddling about trying to change gear and press the clutch. He could just navigate and push it as hard as it would go.
The cars were evenly matched, probably the same model and spec. This meant that at full speed, they wouldn't close the gap on him, but it also meant that he wouldn't be able to pull any distance on them.
They drove fast down the wider road, weaving through the traffic. Taylor pulled into the oncoming lane to overtake cars and then pulled back over to get out of the way of oncoming traffic. It was like a massive

game of chase, only with cars. He couldn't pull a gap, but he had started to recognise signs and places. He saw a sign for a town where he had once had an assignment and knew he was closing in on where he needed to be headed.

He just needed to lose that damn car following him.

He pulled out, realised he had made a mistake as there was a car in the oncoming lane, slammed his brakes on and pulled the wheel to bring the car back where he had come from, but he had lost momentum, and the silver car hit him from behind. It jolted him forward, sending vibrations through his body, making his bones feel the hurt all over again. He was sweating, shaking, and Taylor was worried he would soon descend into shock, but the adrenaline was pushing him forward. He knew once he ran out, though, he was about done.

He took another hit from behind and heard something shatter, maybe the rear light? No, it was the rear window. He knew this when a bullet flew past his head and out through the windscreen; they were now firing at him. He heard bullets embed themselves in the seats, trim, and dings as they hit the bodywork.

Taylor swerved around another car, then pulled sharply back in as an oncoming car blasted its horn and flashed its lights. The silver pursuing car hadn't been able to get around in time, and now, he had a few precious second's grace.

Taylor came up with a plan. He needed to get a gap, and he knew it was a short motorway section before getting on to the winding backroads and to the village he was trying to reach. He knew the motorway junction was close, he knew roughly where it was, and he breathed a sigh of relief when it appeared into his view. The silver pursuit car had, by now, managed to navigate the traffic and was back behind him. The junction was just ahead, and traffic lights were regulating the flow of traffic onto the round-about that was before the access slip road. There were five exits, and Taylor wanted exit four, at his two o'clock as he approached. This would mean waiting at the lights, then driving around from six to two from his position, as it was viewed on a clock, and then another set of lights to allow access to the slip road onto the motorway.

That was too much, too long. Once there was a break in the side barrier Taylor pulled the car onto the grass and ran parallel with the road. Traffic was built up on the road and tailed back, so that meant the only way he could keep any sort of speed was off-roading. Now he was grateful for the 4x4 he was in. He risked a look back, the silver car was mimicking his movement, and they both bounced over the uneven surface, the cars doing their best to give a soft ride, but they were going as fast as they could, and Taylor was being bounced and thrown all over the place. He crashed back into his seat again, groaning at the extra damage his body was being put through, he was tensed up, and every time the car bounced and landed, it ricocheted through him. Taylor was pretty sure he had opened his cut up more as there was a big red patch soaking through his uniform.

He grimaced and wanted to move his hand to cover it, but he needed both on the wheel to maintain control of the car.
He careered onto the roundabout, driving around the traffic lights; he was grateful for the tarmac. He then just pointed the car at the junction and put his foot down. He was going the wrong way around the roundabout, cars were flashing and beeping their horns, but Taylor didn't care. He saw an empty lane and slipped the Range Rover through it, then moved over again, narrowly missing a car that had no idea he was coming. He banked up again onto the grass as the lanes became blocked with cars, people just going about their lives, driving home from work to their families, their food, and their TV. The Range Rover scrambled for grip and propelled him further. He drove around the other set of lights on the grass and then re-emerged on the slip road, forcing a car to emergency break and swerve to avoid hitting him.
He sped down the slip road and joined the main motorway. It was busy, but not too bad, and he weaved through the traffic, the silver car still following, although he had managed to gain a small gap as they had both cut out the roundabout and the lights, but Taylor had been braver and had been rewarded by gaining a slight lead.
He tried to weave and dab his breaks, causing cars to slam theirs on in panic, he hoped to cause a block or the silver car to crash, but the chasing car was able to navigate the obstacles and keep the pressure on. This wasn't working. Taylor moved the Range Rover over

to the hard shoulder and just gunned it. He looked in the mirror, saw something coming out from the car behind, an arm, and then a flash, and another one, and another. They were back to firing at him, but at this speed, with the noise of the engine and the wind racing over the car, he couldn't hear any of them.
The Range Rover sped past 120mph and continued to rise as he pushed everything the car had, the cars on the motorway were blurs as he accelerated, pushing harder, 130mph, 140mph.
Taylor knew he was going too fast. He would need to rid himself of some of this speed if he stood a chance of making the turn, but if he slowed, he would be caught, and if they rammed him again, he would most likely lose control and crash. The junction was approaching, the marker for the first warning to slow down and prepare for the slip road appeared. He looked around. There must be something, something. Anything! There was a break in the traffic, a gap only a few cars long, it was all he had so he let off the accelerator, letting the big car slow naturally, the silver one was coming closer, closer. When it was close enough, he yanked the wheel and swerved back into the traffic. He was now almost on the turning, and as he forced himself back onto the main carriage way cars slammed their brakes on, there was a loud crash, and Taylor glanced back at the accident he had caused, then focused on what he was doing and looked forward.
His plan had worked. The silver car had overshot and sped past him on the hard shoulder; it slammed its

brakes on, but would it get rid of enough speed before the exit?
Taylor was still breaking hard; he could smell the rubber and the brakes as he tried to remove all the Range Rovers momentum. It was enough, and he swerved back onto the hard shoulder and accelerated up the next junction.
There was another roundabout; he wanted to go left at the top of the exit road, so he just mounted the grass again and cut it off. He drove fast, the car picking up past 70mph, 80mph as he drove down the road.
"Where is it…" He said to himself, searching the road as he drove, praying he hadn't got it wrong.
"Where are you…" Taylor muttered under his breath, "…There! Yes!"
A sign for the village, it was the village past this one that he was looking for. He slammed the brakes once again, and he kept checking the rear view to look for the re-appearance of the silver car. He knew it would have turned around and tried to begin the pursuit again, but there had been so many exits and turns they wouldn't know which one, if any, he had taken.
He took the right turning and drove through the village:

Charleston

The sign greeted him as he entered, asking people to *please drive slowly through our village*. Slowing the car down and driving normally, he drove past little cottage houses and local businesses, most closed for the day. He passed a pub at the edge of the village and

entered out onto the back roads. Taylor picked up some speed and knew that he wasn't far away as he cruised the car and navigated the tight, narrow roads until he was at the next village over.
He was still sweating; he was hot and cold at the same time, and the soaked uniform clung to him, but then a thought came into his mind.
If he were Carson, he would have his cars monitored.
Shit.
He needed to ditch the Range Rover; he couldn't take the risk.
He pulled into a small parking area he found near a public park, thought about his plan of action. Once he had decided, Taylor drove on until he found what he needed. Then he stopped in the road. The car was an automatic, and this meant that if no pressure were applied to the brake, the car would move slowly forward as long as it was in drive. He aimed it at the ditch, opened the door, took his foot off the brake and stepped out as the car started to pull itself forward slowly.

It was the first time Taylor had seen it from the outside since he had taken it. The rear window was smashed, both rear lights were shattered, and the boot had been badly dented from the hit. Bullet holes riddled along the bodywork, the wheels had clumps of grass stuck between the spokes as well as in the brakes. It smelt of burnt brakes and rubber, and Taylor thought to himself, as he watched it slowly crawl itself to its ditch grave, pitching forward and then falling in, leaving the destroyed back protruding from the brow of the ditch – *I bet that wasn't what Range Rover had in mind for this when they built it.*

He then turned and started making his way across the fields to the village. He kept low, staying close to the edges and the bushes; after an hour or so, he made it to the village. He walked the streets, trying to keep out of sight, it was dark again now, but even so, Taylor kept to the quieter streets, his body screamed at him to just go straight there, and with every step, he felt weaker. His instincts, however, were to keep low as he didn't want to bring trouble to her door. Eventually, he made it through the winding streets of houses, past the children's play park, the local shop and up a hill that felt like it was the steepest thing he had ever climbed. It wasn't, but in Taylor's state, everything seemed exhausting. He had made it, though. He was at the house.

42

Carson and his driver found the black Range Rover a short while later. It was in a ditch. Carson had turned on the locator once he had lost track of it and had circled around and found it.

"Burn it." Carson had told the driver, and the driver made a call. Within the hour, it would just be a smouldering wreckage, and all evidence would be gone.

He was a man of business, and Carson knew this could come back on him. He killed anybody that put his freedom at risk, and this man was out there, and he could become a problem. Thankfully, he knew how to solve it.

He made a call.

"Hello," an American answered the phone.

"It's Carson. You want my company; you can have it," he said. "For the agreed price, and one more thing. The man you sent. I want him dead. Once he is and I have his body so I can be sure, then it's all yours."

"Hold, please."

Carson was now back in the Range Rover being driven back to the city. He needed to make a stop at his office, and then he would make his arrangements and disappear.

"Thank you for holding," the voice on the phone said. "Your terms have been agreed to. We will be in touch shortly." The line went dead.

They wanted Carson's company; they could have it; all the surface stuff allocated at Geologica Industries. The other stuff, the deeper stuff, the stuff that matters, he would strip away and move. Geologica would be sold, but he would just start up a new business, with a new front, and go back to his ways with his clients unaffected.
Maxwell Carson was a businessman. He would evolve and endure.

Part Three

43

Olivia Swann opened her front door, and a man was standing there, hunched over, using his left arm to support his weight against the wall, and his right was across his chest, holding his side. He was covered in minor, almost healed scratches across his face, a cut lip, black eyes, what looked like a severe ice burn and a crescent moon shaped deep cut around from his eyebrow to his temple.

He looked up at her, started saying something, but then just collapsed on the floor.

She brought him inside.

Logan Taylor opened his eyes. It was dark in here; wherever he was, he tracked his thoughts back.

I was being chased.

The fields.

The streets.

The house. Yes, he had made it to the house.

Then he remembered the door opening, and Olivia was standing there, he had gone to say hello, but all he remembered was his world going black and then nothing. He must have fainted.

He heard a noise as a woman entered the room; he looked around and tried to sit up.

“Don’t, don’t try to get up yet,” Olivia said. “You need to rest.” She was holding a bowl with a liquid inside; he didn’t know what it was. “Take this,” she said. He

did, without question. Olivia knew what she was doing, and he had come here because he trusted her.
Olivia Swann was a nurse, or a doctor, or someone high up who was responsible for caring for and healing broken people. Taylor had come across her on a previous assignment, she was caught up in a situation that was on the edge of his target, and he had helped her remove herself from it.
The man she was in trouble with, his assignment, was no longer breathing.
She had been grateful and said if he ever needed anything, he could come to her. She had a couple of bags of supplies at her house for emergencies, and he was grateful for them today.
Olivia was curvy, and not overly tall. She had long dark blonde hair that was tied up, and her arms were slim. She had brown eyes and a nose piercing in her left nostril. She had tattoos on the tops of her arms showing, placed so that her uniform would easily cover them. She wore jogging trousers and a vest top.
Taylor took a sip of what she gave him, it did not taste good, and his gag reflex wanted to spit it back up, but he forced himself to swallow it.
"Looks like you've been in the wars," Olivia said as she sat on a chair next to him.
"Something like that," he replied, his voice croaky and weak, barely above a whisper.
"You win?" She asked.
"Not yet," Taylor groaned, "but it's not over."

"I think it is, or it should be, you're a mess, Red, and I don't think you should be going back out there for a while."
"Thanks for your concern, doc, but you know I won't be doing that."
He assessed his body, allowed all the aches and pains to be felt. He wanted to know what still worked. Everything hurt. His legs were the best, though; they seemed to have come out relatively ok and just ached. Taylor moved his hand down to the stab wound at his side. It was covered by a square bandage that was taped across it.
"It was infected," said Olivia. "I had to clean it up before I could dress it. You need a hospital really."
"Thanks, doc"
"Most of it seems superficial. Whatever happened to you, you got lucky. Most of it just seems like you took a beating, other than the ice burn on your face. How did that happen, although I think I have an idea?"
"Your idea is either right or better than the truth, so just stick with that."
"It will heal." She explained, "there is a nasty cut above your eye that's going to scar, nothing I can do about that, same as the one on your chest. Other than that, it just seems like bruised ribs, black eyes, cuts, and bruises. But I can only see what's on the outside and feel a little of what's going on inside. You could have some serious damage. You really should get help."
Taylor had wounds already on his body. He had two bullet wounds on his legs and one on his shoulder, just

next to the shoulder blade that had healed over. He had a scar down his calf from when a man in a jungle had captured him and tried to skin him, which had also healed, along with other small scars from wounds he had sustained over his careers.

“I did. I came here.” Taylor smiled weakly.

“More help, in a hospital.”

“Doc?”

“Yes?”

“Why am I naked?”

“I needed to check you over, and those clothes you had on were soaked and were probably the cause of your infection, so I had to take them off, and I needcd to make sure I could tend to all your wounds.”

“Ok.”

“Relax, it's nothing I haven’t seen before. You’ve got nothing I’m interested in anyway.”

“Harsh.”

“If you’re that bothered, I’ll get you a sheet.” She got up, left the room, and he heard her go upstairs.

Taylor looked around. He was lying on a sheet covering a leather sofa in a cream room with wood accents in the furniture. There was a patterned carpet on the floor, a chair next to the sofa, angled toward him so that it looked like she was a therapist. There was a small artificial fire built into the chimney breast, and pictures decorated the walls.

He heard her come down the stairs, and Olivia came back in with a duvet cover and tossed it over to him.

“Here ya go.”

"Thanks," he said and placed it lightly over himself.
"I'll be out of your hair soon. How long was I out?"
"A few hours. Red, listen, I know you won't listen, but I seriously don't recommend going back after whoever it is your planning on going after until you are a lot, lot, stronger."
"Thanks for the advice, doc."
"But you're going to ignore it?"
He just looked at her.
"Ok fine, but at least give me a day. Some stuff at the hospital will help you, even if only short term, and then you can do whatever you want. Ok?"
Taylor thought about it; he wanted to get up and leave now, he had been patched up, and he wanted to take the fight to Carson as soon as possible. However, he knew what he would be up against, and Carson would get more men around him for protection in case Taylor came after him.
"Ok." He nodded.
"Promise me, Red."
"I promise, scouts honour. Do you have a phone?"

Taylor called Edgar, but no answer; he knew there wouldn't be because of The Company policy, never answered unknown numbers first time, secure the line, and called them back.
Olivia's phone rang from a blocked number, he answered it.
"Hi, Edgar, it's Red,"
"RED! Oh, thank god you're ok. I've been looking for you everywhere, man. What the hell happened?"

"I'm ok."
"You sure, man? You don't sound it." Edgar's voice sounded concerned.
"Ed, I'm fine. But the contract has become complicated."
"Yeah, it has, in a way," Edgar interrupted. "It's been cancelled because you didn't fulfil it. The admin lady wants you back here so she can talk to you. Where are you?"
"Close. Ed, the guy tried to kill me."
Edgar dragged the word "Shit" out so that it lasted over a second.
"I need you to cover for me, tell them I'm on my way; I'm just tying up some loose ends. Can you do that for me?
"I dunno, man, I don't want to piss 'em off, y'know."
"I'll clear it all up when I get back," Taylor assured him.
"Ok, man," Edgar sighed, "but how long will you need?"
"Forty-eight hours, maybe a little more."
"Ok. But I want a check-in after then, or I'm bailing and telling them, deal?"
"Deal."
Taylor hung up the phone, and when Olivia came back in, he handed it back to her. She sat in the chair. "So, you're really going to do this?"
"Yes."
"Then get some rest. Once I'm back from work tomorrow, I'll do a final dress change, and you can be on your way."

"Thank you, Liv. You got any men's clothes lying around?"
"Boy, do I look like the kind of girl that has guys clothes lying around?"
"Maybe."
She smiled, "Well, I don't. You know I prefer my company in the form of the better looking of the species." She winked and left the room, calling back, "get some sleep; I'll wake you in the morning."

44

The woman had been staking out the house all day. This was getting ridiculous. Had Carson moved or something? What was taking so long?
Then her phone rang, an American number.
She answered, "hello."
"Hello, there has been a change of plans. Carson is no longer to be the subject."
"What? Why? I've been here for bloody hours."
"An agreement has been made with Mr Carson. You are now to remove the third-party player, as directed by The Chairman."
"OK, fine." She hung up. What deal had been made? She had missed something, but it didn't matter, she got up and went back to the BMW and thought about her next move.
She had two options from what she saw. The man may try and come back and take out Carson out of principal for having not being able to convince him to sell, or he would go back to where he had come from. But he didn't have a car.
Would he borrow one?
What about his stuff? It seemed unlikely he would have put it all back in his car before going to see Carson. The apartment – flat – block kept coming into her mind. She took a hunch, started the car up and drove back to the flats.

45

Taylor was woken in the morning by Olivia's voice bringing him around. She had a pleasant voice and a good bedside manner. His eyes adjusted, focused on seeing her standing over him; she held a glass of water and some pills.

"Morning," Olivia said softly.

"Morning," he replied. His voice was coming back to him now and getting stronger.

"Take these," she gave the pills and the water to him. "Then I'll change your dressings before I go to work."

"Thank you, doc." He said as he swallowed the pills and finished off the water.

His body was still weak, still sore, but he felt a world better than he had done twenty-four hours ago.

She changed the bandages on his stomach, chest and above his eye, cleaning the wounds as she did so. It stung as the cleaner touched his damaged skin. He took a sharp intake of breath and flinched.

"Baby," Olivia said as she carried on.

Once done, she brought him more water and some food.

"Rest," she said. "Once I'm back from work, I'll be able to get you up enough to at least attempt what you want to do."

"Thanks again, doc," Taylor said as he eased himself back down onto the sofa. If he was honest, he

welcomed a few more hours of rest. His mind and body were exhausted and needed to re-charge.
He heard her leave to go to work, and within minutes his body had told him to go back to sleep, to rest. Recover. Repair it seemed to be saying to him.
So, he listened. He slept.

As Taylor slept, a black BMW parked up in the same spot around the corner from the flats as it had before. She had parked a little closer this time so she could watch from the car as the first few drops of water landed on the windscreen from the first signs of rain. She waited.

Taylor awoke at the sound of a noise, a disturbance. He was about to get up when he heard Olivia's voice announcing her return from work. The sun was setting, and it was now raining. He had been asleep all day.
She came in, wearing similar clothes to what she had worn the night before, and she was carrying bags.
"I got the stuff; I also went clothes shopping for you."
She placed the bags on the table in the kitchen. It was visible through the living room door.
"Really? Thank you," Taylor said. She pulled out some doctor's scrubs and held them up against herself to show him.
"What do you think?"
"That'll work, thank you. Can you drop me off at the flat I'm staying in? I have a change of clothes and some weapons still there. I need to go there before I go back."

"Ok," she said. "Same place as last time? I'll change your dressing, and then if you still feel you're going to go, I'll take you. Still don't recommend it, though."
Taylor knew he wasn't perfect, far from it, but he was feeling better, and he knew no matter what, he was having his rematch with Carson, only this time he wouldn't be tied up.
"Thank you," was all he said and sat himself up.

An hour or so later, Taylor was pretty much ready to leave Olivia's house. He was still hurting, but he knew if he waited too long, Carson might become hard to find, and Taylor didn't want to miss his chance at payback.
It was his ego, he knew it, but he was still going to do it.

Olivia opened the bag and took out some boxes of tablets. She took some out of each box, gave them to him with a glass of water and told him to take them.
"What are they?" He asked.
"Would you know if I told you?" She replied.
Fair point, he thought and took them, then washed them down.
She then took out a needle and a small vial with a clear liquid in it.
"What's that?"
"Something to help keep you strong, think of it as adrenaline in a bottle; it will keep you moving, help dull any pains you have and help you push through any new ones."

"Ok," said Taylor. "Great."
"When this is done, you go to a hospital. You hear me?"
"Yes, ok, fine."
"This will keep you going for a good few hours."
"How much can I have?"
"I'm giving you enough; if I give you too much, there's a risk of it being too much for your heart."

After she had injected him, Taylor felt like he was on a sugar high. He got dressed in the scrubs, and they got into her grey Fiat, and she drove him as he directed her to the block of flats.

As they pulled up, they drove past a black BMW that sat on the corner, and even though Taylor only caught a glance as they passed, there looked to be someone in the driver's seat.
They parked in the space allocated, the one he had been using for his Jaguar, and he turned to Olivia.
"Thank you."
"You're welcome. I'll wait here."
"No, it's ok. You have done enough; I don't want to drag you further into this." Taylor insisted.
"How will you get wherever you need to go?"
"I'll steal a car."
"Look, just let me help you. I'll drive you to where you need to go, I'll stay out of the way, and I'll drive you out once you're done."
Taylor looked at her, and she looked back at him. The look in her eye showed she was just as stubborn as he

was. He didn't want her involved, but it was his fault for going to her in the first place, and she was probably one of only a few people he could call a friend.
"Ok, fine," he said. "But stay here until I come back. Understand?"
"Yes."
Taylor got out of the car, hobbled up to the door and went inside. He went up to Flat 5 and listened through the door. The TV was still on, which was a good thing, as it meant no one was in there, or a bad thing because someone was, and they were waiting in there knowing he would think it was clear, come in and then they would shoot him.
He had lost his key, along with everything else he had on him when he had been grabbed at Carson's house. So, he used the hairpins he had borrowed from Olivia, knowing he would need to break in, and jimmied the door open. He slowly went inside; it was empty. No one was waiting for him. It was ok.

The woman sat in the BMW across the street waited a moment before she made her move. She got out of the car, the rain now latching onto her clothes as she walked over to the grey Fiat that had just pulled up and knocked on the window. The woman inside jumped, raised her hand to her chest and pressed the button, and the window buzzed down.
The woman leaned down. "Hi, I'm looking for my friend, I work with him, but he's been missing," she said, making her voice as soft and delicate as she could

as the rain ran down her face and amplified her angular features as the drops followed the lines of her face.
"You know Red?" Olivia asked.
"Red, hm, yes, Red, that's it. Is he ok?"
"He's inside."
The woman looked at the front of the car; there was a sign that said:

Allocated parking:
5

The woman straightened up and dropped her voice back to her original tone, and the American accent came back through. "Great, thanks," she said. Then she drew her pistol from the small of her back and shot her.

Then the woman walked through the rain and into the building, up the stairs and towards Flat 5.

46

Taylor was gathering his things, he needed everything, but he had decided he would freshen up and get changed. The light, thin material of the scrubs meant he was cold, and they didn't feel natural with just his underwear underneath them. He needed his suit.

He was just getting ready to get changed when there was a knock at the door. He turned and looked at the source; it was probably Olivia, coming up to try and be helpful.

He hadn't told her what flat he was in, but they had parked in the allocated parking, so it wouldn't take much to figure it out.

He moved to the door and looked through the hole.

It wasn't Olivia. It was another woman.

As Taylor looked through, the woman took a step back, brought up her gun, and Taylor had just enough time to throw himself to the side before bullets came through the door. He hit the ground and turned just as the door was kicked open and the woman walked in.

"Oh, this is the place," she said. "Good. I didn't shoot the lady for nothing."

He recognised her. She had an angular yet soft face and features he recognised. It was the woman from The White Lion.

What was going on?

Had she been following him?

Now she was trying to kill him!

She turned to him, and he charged her, taking her off her feet, and they went tumbling to the floor.

She kicked him off, and he rolled, rose to one knee, and a foot came swinging at him. Taylor raised his arm to block and took the brunt of the blow, forcing him down, but he used the momentum to turn and get himself to his feet. She was in front of him again, throwing punches, and he raised his arms like a defending boxer absorbing what he could. She was forcing him back further into the room, towards the bedroom at the back. He tried to make a stand, but she kicked him hard in the side, narrowly missing the knife wound. However, it still sent a surge of pain through his body. As Taylor dropped to his left knee, she whipped her knee up to try and hit him in the face, but he used both hands to block and then drive his right elbow into her stomach, this winded her, and she was forced to take a step back, as she did so he punched her in the stomach again. Taylor had gained a brief advantage and needed to push it home. He rose again, now on the attack, the woman swung with a right hook, he grabbed it, turned, and threw her over his hip. She hit the floor but wrapped her legs around his arm, and she took him down with her.

Taylor broke her hold, and she struck with her foot, he managed to keep distance from her, but she once again had the advantage. She was up, and now there was a knife in her hand, and she slashed at him, he kept out of the way, as she struck again, Taylor grabbed her wrist that held the knife, punched her in the chest and used his heel to strike at her knee cap. The crunch as it

made contact was loud, and she screamed, dropping the knife, but she stayed up, punching him in the face and pulling her wrist free.
There was a moments stand-off. She stood there, all her weight on her good leg, evil hatred in her eyes, and her hands raised.
Taylor looked at her. She was wearing all black with a brown leather jacket.
Who was she?
She sounded American.
Why was she here?
Was she one of Carson's people? Was she sent to track him down?
It didn't matter. She said she had shot the lady; did she mean Olivia? He needed to get downstairs and check on her.
The woman snarled and came at him again. She seemed to feel no fear, and he wasn't the only one pumped with adrenaline. Taylor met her with a kick that sent her reeling, and as she got up, he moved in, punched her in the face with his right hand, blocked her right with his left, kicked her other knee out from under her and punched her in the throat.
She went down, coughing and gasping for air. Then, somehow, she started to get back up.
This had to end, now. She had picked up the knife and came at him, Taylor moved, but he felt the blade pass through the loose scrubs he was wearing. He grabbed her hand, twisted it, and broke her wrist. She howled in pain and backed off, pulling her broken arm up to her chest and prepared to come again.

“Seriously?” Taylor exclaimed,
“I will kill you.” She breathed.
He was stood next to her gun; it was at his feet. He looked down; she did the same. He moved first, bent down, and grabbed it as she came at him. Taylor turned and fired. The bullet ripped through the air, found the knee that was already broken and shattered the bone. The force took the leg out from under her, and she fell forward, screaming in pain, hitting the floor face first. She growled through gritted teeth at him, like a wounded animal that was still determined to kill its prey as she started dragging herself across the floor towards her knife. Taylor walked over, kicked the blade out of her reach. She growled again and rolled onto her back.
She looked up at him.
He looked down at her.
“Did you kill my friend?” Taylor asked.
She started laughing, a deep painful laugh, as if she were remembering how funny it was through the pain she was feeling.
Taylor shot her in her shoulder; she stopped laughing and cried out as he asked,
“Who sent you?”
She said nothing.
Taylor shot her in her other shoulder. She cried out again.
Blood was soaking into the brown carpet, it hid it well, but it was definitely coming out from her wounds.
“Who. Sent. You?” He said slowly, placed his foot on the broken knee and applied the smallest amount of

pressure, and she cried out in pain. Tears ran down her face. She looked like a wounded animal, but she never answered.

"Last time. Then I'm going to kill you. Who sent you here? Carson?"

Then she spoke, it was broken words, she was in a lot of pain, she spat blood as she said "you… know," then paused and grimaced at her pain before she carried on, "if you're going to kill someone, just do it." Then she spat on him, the blood staining the legs of the scrubs he was wearing.

"I usually do take that approach," Taylor said as he knelt beside her. She weakly flailed her good arm at him, trying to still fight him somehow. He grabbed it, pinned it to the floor with his foot and shot through her hand.

She screamed.

"But," he said, "I want to know if someone is after me. Is there?"

She was getting whiter and whiter as the blood escaped through her wounds. She was losing consciousness and possibly about to enter shock from all the trauma her body had endured.

She whispered, "Carson," it was quiet and seemed like it may be the last word she would ever say. Her head was slowly moving from side to side, her eyes rolling around in her head as she was desperately trying to stay alive.

Taylor straightened up, looked down at her.

Then he delivered the final shot.

The woman had told herself ever since she had arrived that she would be leaving. She wouldn't be stuck in this country, this horrible, rainy, backwards, floating rock. She would never give up the Chairman or anything on the Committee, but this guy wanted a name, so why not give him one he already had? He was already after Carson, so why not just give him more fuel to add to the fire.

As she lay there, on the dirty carpeted floor of that flat, her body trying to keep itself working, desperately trying to pump blood around her system, but failing, her life fading away, she clung to the thought of America. Home. The greatest country in the world.

She would never see it again.

She wasn't getting out.

She would never go home.

She was going to be in England forever.

She heard the rain clatter against the window, the rain of England, and she saw the man stand up, loom over her. She saw the gun, her gun, pointed down at her.

She never left England.

47

Taylor left the woman there, lying on the floor and ran down the stairs. He burst out the front door to the flats and saw the grey Fiat still parked. The rain had become heavier, the scrubs were light and thin and were soaked through in seconds, they stuck and clung to his skin, and his hair was plastered to his scalp. He ran to the car, water splashing from the puddles and soaking his shoe protectors that were acting as actual shoes for him.

The driver's window was open, and as he rounded the car, he saw Olivia slumped in the driver's seat. There was blood covering the seat she was sitting in and sprayed around the interior. As Taylor gently lifted her head, he saw the bullet hole in her forehead.

She was gone.

"I'm so sorry, Liv," He wept, "I'm so sorry." He was glad it was raining. It disguised the tears that ran down his cheeks as he stood there for a moment, leaning down against the car. He decided in that moment.

Taylor opened the car door and lifted her out. He carried her into the building, praying no one came out. Thankfully, they didn't, and he reached Flat 5. The door was hanging off its hinges, and after he brought her in and placed her on the sofa, he went back and put it back as best he could.

He used the toilet and took a shower, taking the dressings off, the kick he had taken during the fight had distressed his wound, and it was soaked in blood. Once out of the shower, Taylor used the dressings he had brought with him initially, they were similar, square material with adhesive tape along each edge, but these were thinner and not as good.
He didn't re-dress his eye. He just cleaned it as best he could and left the cut exposed. He didn't want to risk the dressing coming loose and impairing his vision; he wasn't as good at dressing wounds as Olivia was.
Had been.

He dragged the American woman, whoever she was, into the bathroom and dumped her in the shower. Then he carefully carried Olivia to the bed and placed her on it. Other than the entry wound and how white she was, she could have been sleeping.
He shouldn't have brought her into this.

It was time to end it.

Taylor got dressed in an all-black, three-piece suit, the lining of the jacket and the back of his waistcoat, this time being a dark crimson red, matched his tie.
He put his shoes on and went to pick up his watch.
Carson had taken his watch and his phone. *Bastard.*
He went to the woman in the shower cubicle, searched her pockets, unzipped her jacket, and checked the inside pockets.
There was a phone and keys.
Great.

He called Edgar. No answer. He put the phone down and finished checking and loading his weapons, then the phone rang.
"Hello, Edgar,"
"Red? Oh, good to hear your voice, man. You done? You on your way back?"
"Nearly, I need you to search this phone I'm calling you on if you can. I need to know about the owner. Who she is, and how she found me?"
"Ok, I shouldn't, but I will. Why not just ask her?"
"She's dead."
"That would do it, yeah, Ok, leave the phone on, and leave it with me."
"Ed."
"Yeah?"
"How long will it take you to disable everything in Carson's house? So you have full control."
"A while, why?"
"Because in an hour or so, I'll be paying him a visit, and I want him to be completely shut off, isolated. No phones, no signals, no security. Nothing."
"Ok. I'll see what I can do. Everything ok, you sound pissed."
"That's because I am."
"I would not want to be Mister Carson right now," Edgar whispered.
"No, you would not." Taylor couldn't keep the anger out of his voice. "One more thing."
"What?"
"Flat 5 is burnt. Need immediate containment and removal of two female bodies. The door also isn't

attached properly anymore, so it's exposed, need it done fast."
"Done. But this may bring it to peoples attention you don't want right now."
"Doesn't matter. Edgar, the woman on the bed, was a friend, see she is looked after accordingly."
"Ok, sure," Edgar's voice was sincere. "What about the other one?"
"I.D her and burn her."
Taylor hung up and put the phone in his pocket. He also took Olivia's phone. If there was a chance someone was listening on the woman's, even on the secure lines The Company could set up; there was no way they would be on Olivia's.
He picked up the keys, saw they were for a BMW.
"I wonder," he muttered under his breath.
He finished packing and took all this stuff downstairs. He planned on taking Olivia's car, but then he had a thought.
Taylor tapped the unlock button, and the black BMW on the corner's indicators flashed. He walked over.
"Bitch," he muttered. He was sure it was the one that had been following him around. He should have been paranoid. He might have spotted her sooner, dealt with her then.
If so, Olivia would still be alive.

Taylor put his stuff in the boot of the BMW and got in the driver's seat, the rain-soaked clothes squeaking against the black leather. He slid the seat back and noticed there was a laptop on the passenger seat. He opened it up, but it was locked. He had no idea where to start with it, so he just closed it back down. That would be a job for Edgar when they were back at the studio.

Taylor engaged the sat nav. The car had been to many of the same places he had. Carson's house, the office, the flats, but there was no showing of the industrial estate. There was a marker for a random field, though, strange.

He started the car, it was dark, and the lights came on automatically as the wipers engaged themselves to clear the rain from the windscreen. He set off towards Carson's house.

48

Taylor arrived at Carson's house in forty-five minutes. He had been driving fast. He wanted to get this over with.

He pulled up and dialled Edgar and waited for him to call back. The rain was still pouring heavily outside, and he wondered if it was just God mirroring his mood and emotions and thought the rain would be a good way of doing so.

He didn't believe in God per se, but he hoped there was something after this; it was a comforting thought that Olivia would be somewhere better. The girl from the abandoned unit too, and all the others he had seen die around him that shouldn't have or didn't deserve to.

The phone rang.

"You ready?" Taylor said as he answered.

"I am, yeah, but Carson's not in there," Edgar informed him.

"What? Then where is he?"

"Don't know. He left shortly after your talk with him; then I got nothing on him coming back."

"Shit. Ok, keep an eye on this place and have a look at his office. He may be there."

"He was; he came and went. Then I lost track of him. Maybe he went somewhere without cameras. I don't know."

Somewhere without cameras. Taylor thought.

“Ok. I think I know where he is. The unit. I’ll try there.” He hung up, put the car back in drive and set off again into the dark, rain-stained night.

Taylor arrived at the unit and parked the BMW around the corner of the next unit along. Lights were flashing around erratically inside, must be hand torches. He slowly got out; gently pressed the door closed so the clunk wouldn’t alert anyone.
He drew his backup weapon, his Glock 26 – his 34 had also been taken upon his abduction – and moved to the door.
He was pumped, he was ready, he could feel that whatever Olivia had given him was dulling most of his pain, but he knew it was still there. He had to be fast and methodical. It was a big open space, and he didn’t want to be caught in the open in the middle of it.
He could hear voices inside, three, maybe four. He breathed deep, pulled his gun close to his chest, tactical breach. Hopefully quietly.
The rain was tapping on the corrugated roof, making most of the noise, its relentless pattern hiding his movements. Taylor slowly opened the door, just enough to peak his head and his gun around - if anyone was there, he needed to be ready - his blood was pumping, his mind was focused, he pushed out the images of when he had been here last; it would be different this time.
It was clear. Men were walking around, moving things towards the far end of the unit. He slipped inside and hid behind the first pillar he came too. He waited,

anticipating bullets to fire in his direction or shouting if he had been seen.
Nothing.
He breathed, composed himself.
He glanced around. It was clear. From the light beams of the moon coming in through the damaged roof, he could see two men on the ground floor, one in the office upstairs.
If they weren't Carson, he needed one alive to tell him where he was. He moved out and slowly crept up to the next concrete pillar. His gun pointed ahead just in case things went bad. There was debris on the floor and loose items lying around, but hc avoided stepping on them, the rain covering the already faint sounds of his canvas shoes on the floor.
He hid behind the next pillar with his back up against it.
He glanced around again.
One guard was moving something to the back of the bottom office, and one was collecting things up and moving them around. It looked like they were just cleaning up. The light in the bottom office was on, but the bulb was weak and didn't give much away about the men. What he did know, however, was that neither of them was Carson.
Maybe upstairs?
The guard on the unit floor was moving aimlessly around. Taylor kicked a piece of metal, it clanged, and he heard confused noises.
"Hey, you hear that?" One shouted.
"No, what?"

"Nothing."
Taylor heard the faint sound of footsteps approaching; He was listening hard for sound and could hear someone get closer. One of the men was on the other side of the pillar.
Then the movement stopped.
Now or never.
Taylor swung around the pillar. The guard had just turned and had his back to him, so Taylor grabbed him in a chokehold and held him, applied pressure until his brain shut down, and he passed out, then dragged him behind the pillar, so it was harder to see him.
One down. Two to go.
He had taken longer than he would have liked with the hold; the muscles in his arms were still weak.
Need to remember that, he told himself.
He moved up and kept low. The man in the bottom office had his back to him, and the light beam was weak upstairs, so whoever was up there wasn't in the front office.
The man upstairs could be Carson. He knew the one downstairs wasn't. Part of his brain said to take out the man downstairs, then move upstairs. But if the man downstairs saw him and made a noise, the man upstairs had the high ground, and there was only one way up. Taylor chose to go up, and he moved to the stairs, keeping quiet, with his gun trained on the man in the office, just in case he turned as he passed. Taylor glanced at the spot where the girl had been lying. It was dark, and he couldn't make out if she were still there or not. He reached the stairs and took a breath,

and then he started to head up, being as quiet as he could against the metal. His trousers were wet and clung to his legs, making it harder to move as he would like. He reached the top and looked down the hall to the left. In the end office, the flashlight beam bounced lazily around the room, the carrier clearly bored and just pacing.

He turned the corner and hid in the first office space. He looked around again; it was clear, so he moved to the open doorway in the second office. The next one was the end office. He kept low, wincing at the pain the position put on his wounds, but he pressed on and found the guard sitting in an office chair in the corner with his back to the door, his face half-lit up at the front from a phone screen light. He was swaying slightly; that was what was causing the flashlight beam to wave lazily. His machine gun was on the table.

Taylor paced silently up behind him, the carpet and the rain completely drowning out his footsteps.

Taylor aimed the barrel of his gun at the man's head. He had short-shaved hair, and he looked stocky from the angle he had, but he wasn't Carson.

Taylor touched the barrel to the back of his head as he said in a low voice, "your friends are dead. Scream if you want, but it'll only make you join them."

The guard froze, then nodded.

"Where's Carson?" Taylor asked quietly.

"I don't know. He told us to clean this place up and then guard it. We've been here all day just doing stuff."

"Where would he be if not here, work or his house?"

"I don't know, maybe, maybe the Den?"

The Den sounded familiar. Taylor had a vague memory of hearing it before. Actually, when he was here before, Carson took a call and said he was going to the Den.

“Where is it?”

“I don’t kn...”

The guard was cut off when a voice from downstairs shouted, “are you both up there? Have you both just left me here doing everything?” The man’s posture changed, realising he wasn’t the last man; he turned in his chair and reached for his gun.

Taylor shot him in the head, and as he died, he fell out of the chair and hit the floor.

The gunshot rang out like a thunderbolt into the night, the noise amplified by the relative silence of the surroundings. Taylor heard the man below run up the stairs, and he grabbed the machine gun from the table and took cover under the office window as the man emerged from the stairwell and started firing. The glass above Taylor shattered as bullets ripped through it, and the glass rained down on him.

When there was a break, Taylor lifted up, aimed through the now empty window and returned fire. It was loud, so loud and each crack from their guns echoed around the building, making it sound like a symphony of bangs and bullets.

The man was in an awkward angle and tried to move out into the corridor to the end office to get a better position. As he moved, Taylor lifted, saw it and opened fire. He hit the man in the shoulder and the leg, but he kept moving back. He was now behind the desk in the

office that overlooked the unit space. Taylor knew he needed to close the gap, and he moved up, keeping low and firing in the general direction, just so it meant the guard couldn't, and gave himself cover fire until he ducked into the empty office.
The guard returned fire, and when there was a break, Taylor moved forward again. He was now in the office next to the stairwell. The guard had run out of bullets, Taylor heard the gun try to fire, but the 'click' meant no bullets were left to fire. He raised his weapon to his eye line, moved out and towards the office the last guard was hiding in. The guard had only a handgun and had used his bullets too quick.
The guard tried to jump out from behind the desk but showed his hand too soon. Taylor depressed the trigger, and the machine gun spat bullets that hit him in the chest, blood came out, and he knew he wasn't wearing body armour. The savagery of being hit that many times, that close forced the guard back to the window, he was dead, but before he could slump, Taylor moved in and kicked him out of the shattered window. It wasn't necessary, and it served no purpose. He was already dead, and the kick was pure frustration. Taylor was angry Carson wasn't here either and needed to vent it.
The guard fell and hit the concrete ground below with a thud. A small cloud of dust rose around him, and a pool of blood began seeping out from his body as the dust drifted down and settled once again.

49

After another look around revealed nothing new, nothing that was of any use to him anyway. Taylor walked over and looked at the spot where the woman had been. There was a patch of deep red where her blood had soaked into the concrete where she had been laying, but she wasn't there. She had been moved, and there was nothing left but this stained piece of concrete that showed she was ever here.

He left and got back in the BMW. Where would Carson be? He looked again at her laptop, he knew he couldn't get into it, but he was running out of ideas. Maybe he should go back and just steak out his house. He would have to go back home at some time, surely. But a man with Carson's money and resources, he could slip away, and it could take ages to get on his trail. By then, he may be too far to be able to track. There had to be something.
He called Edgar.
"Hello."
"Ed, has Carson come back to his house yet? Or shown up at the office while it's closed for the night?"
"No, nothing yet."
"Damn it. Ok."
Then an idea came to him, and Taylor started up the BMW and activated the sat nav, loaded up previous

locations and saw the stop the woman had made to a random field.
"I think I may have something," he said. "I'll call you back." He hung up the phone and selected for the car to take him to the destination. He set off, once again, into the night.

When the navigation told Taylor he had arrived, he was in a field. There were some barns down an access road he had seen on the way in, but that was about it. Maybe this was the Den?
He reversed the car back and turned it around, so it was facing back the way he had come, in case of needing a swift exit.
He got out, the mud squelched under his feet, and as he started walking, the mud caked the bottom of his shoes, and every few steps, the mud would stick, threatening to pull his shoe off, but he had them laced tight and was able to get them out and push on easy enough.
The rain wasn't helping; he was getting soaked. But it didn't matter; finding Carson was all that mattered.
Taylor made his way up the access road, keeping to the side, staying as low as he could, his weapon poised and ready in case anyone came out the barn and found him. He reached the first barn, peered in through the sliver that was open, seeing if he could see anyone; he couldn't. He couldn't hear anyone either. He paused before he entered, making sure his feet wouldn't get stuck on the way in and give him away. He pushed the barn door as quietly as he could; it still creaked and resisted being opened, but once he was in, Taylor could

see there was nothing in here other than a car that looked like it had been there for a long time, maybe years.
The floor was dry in here, and other than a few drips, it was well covered. The rain sounded loud on the roof overhead, and after a quick look around, he found nothing of interest to him and no sign Carson had been here. It was hard to judge if anyone had been walking in here though, there were thousands of footsteps, but the uneven dirt and mud floor had kept them preserved so they could be a few hours old or a few months.
He checked that the coast was clear and left, entering into the world and the rain that soaked it. He moved up to the second barn and repeated; he looked at what he could see, the door was much further open, and he could see a couple of burnt-out cars that looked like hatchbacks. He listened but was only rewarded by the sound of the rain. Then he entered, checking his corners and making sure it was clear before he stopped to take in what he had found.
There were two burnt out 4x4's in here, along with the smaller hatchbacks. They both looked freshly destroyed, and he was pretty sure one was his Jaguar F-Pace SVR.
Everything around this Carson assignment just got murdered, Taylor thought, and he would be glad when this one was done. He could just walk away now; he had no obligation to kill Carson as part of the assignment, but Carson had had people killed, people Taylor cared about had been killed, he had destroyed his car, and he had tried to have Taylor himself killed.

No, Maxwell Carson would die tonight.
But he knew this wasn't the Den he was looking for; he was missing something.
He looked at the other 4x4. It looked to be the black Range Rover he had used to escape the unit in; even after the fire had done its best to remove it all, there were still small indications of the damage it had taken when he had been driving it.
There was something on the back seat, and it looked like a body. Taylor moved closer and peered through the hole that was once the rear window, he looked down and the mutilated figure lying across the back seats.
It was the woman from the unit. She was severely burned. She smelt much the same as Houton had after the explosion, this fire had burnt itself out, but the stench of burning still hung in the air. Her flesh looked like something out of a horror movie and had been disfigured so he couldn't make out any of her facial features; but as with the car, the fire couldn't hide everything, and he could see some of the deeper wounds that had survived, and although he couldn't be 100% sure, he was sure enough it was her.
Had Carson killed her because she had been there when Taylor had gone to his house?
Was this his fault?
Taylor put that thought out of his mind and just focused on getting to Carson.
He looked around, but again he couldn't find anything that gave him any clues. He was running out of ideas.
He left the barn and began walking back to the car.

He heard squelching behind him, footsteps. He turned to see two men round the corner. They were hunched over from the rain, wearing uniforms, and carrying small machine guns. They were surprised to see him, not expecting anyone to be there; they were talking when they saw him and were slow to react. Taylor raised his gun and shot them both twice in the chest. They dropped backwards, tiny eruptions of blood came from each wound, and they landed in the mud.

A bullet flew past him, he heard the whistle over the rain, and he turned one hundred and eighty degrees and dropped as he did so. Taylor landed on his back in the mud, his momentum caused him to slide an inch, but as he had done so, he had fired twice more, hitting the guard that had appeared behind him with both bullets, he too, fell backwards off his feet and landed on the floor.

Taylor waited a breath, he would expect them both to be in teams of two, so there should be one more, and sure enough, a moment later, another man came round the corner, his gun raised, surveying the scene, looking for the last man standing, but no one was. He was looking at the wrong height, and Taylor shot him. He fell, just like the others.

Taylor slowly got up, mud now clinging to his jacket and the back of his trousers. He walked over to the bodies, searched each one, looked at the phones that weren't locked, but they didn't provide anything new. He made sure all the men were dead and went back to the BMW.

He opened the trunk and reloaded his Glock.

He was out of ideas. He had nowhere to go, nowhere else to hunt this bastard. His only hope was steaking out the house. That was a long shot.

He climbed back in the BMW, the mud on his back and his legs felt weird against the leather.

He was tired, he was spent, he had been everywhere he could think of, and Carson was nowhere. He had illuded him.

He called Edgar.

"Any news on his properties?"

"No, sorry. Where you trying next?"

"I'll have to stake out the house. That's the only play I have left."

"No joy at the other unit either, then?"

"No, I have been back to the unit I was held in and found a place out in a field, but it's just a dump site. Hang on, what second unit?"

"Before, I found that second unit, remember? In the other industrial estate, but you said not to worry about it because you had decided to use his house instead?"

Taylor had completely forgotten about that; maybe that was the Den!

"Edgar, send me the address for that second unit. Now."

"Ok, sending," Edgar paused, "you should have it."

Olivia's message notification went off, and a glimmer of hope, a spark of possibility ignited in Taylor's stomach.

"Thank you, Ed." He said as he hung up, put the address in the sat nav; it wasn't too far away, a fifteen-minute drive. Perfect.

He arrived in seven minutes. It was late, the roads were quiet, and he did well above what the speed limit told him to do. He was close. He wasn't going to let this guy get away, not now.

The unit looked much the same as the one he had been held in. It was in amongst other units that also seemed to be unused. He could see no lights inside, he couldn't see or hear any movement, but he knew that didn't mean it was empty.

Maybe he was in there, waiting for him.

Taylor was happy for Carson to be waiting for him. He was just sorry it had taken him this long to catch up to him. He knew he needed to gain the upper hand, though, as there could be a lot of men inside waiting to greet him.

He went in the boot of the BMW, opened up one of his bags and withdrew his AR-15 machine gun. He placed his Glock in the small of his back, checked the ammunition and the functions of the AR-15. Once satisfied, he moved back to the door.

Taylor needed a distraction; he needed the first guard to come out.

He found a piece of rock on the floor; this would be perfect, then he got himself in position. When he was ready, he threw the rock at the BMW, smashing the driver's side rear window. In the quiet, the crash sounded like an explosion. If anyone was inside, this should draw them out.

The moon was bright and lit up the area with a luna glow that bathed everything in a blue tone. The rain pattering down on the rooftops sounded tinny, and he thought for a second, he had got it wrong, that no one was there.

Then the door rattled as it opened.

A man exited and looked towards the source of the noise. He was wearing the same security outfit and cap as the others and held a gun lightly in his grip down by his side – lousy tradecraft.

Taylor shot him once through the back in the stomach, and he paced towards him, the loud crack of the rifle echoing through the air. The guard stumbled and dropped his gun. Taylor grabbed him with his left hand on the guard's left shoulder before he could react and placed the gun on his right, using him as a human shield and pushing him back inside.

There were seven men by his count, and the guard was facing them all, protecting the guy they were supposed to kill.

The others had prepared themselves when the guard had gone to look out and had their weapons drawn and ready.

The unit was similar in size to the one he had been kept in but was in much better condition. There were offices upstairs and a similar-sized concrete workspace on the ground floor.

The guards had been ready for someone; once the smash and then the crack of the rifle had been heard, there was no doubt someone was coming. However, seeing their friend facing back at them caused them to hesitate. Taylor had banked on this; people don't just fire bullets into their friends in the real world. They have a moment where their mind panics. Taylor used this moment to open fire. The bullets ripped from the machine gun, and the guard's shoulder jolted back under the recoil. The grip for the second hand had been hooked over, and it would be doing some real damage to the guard's shoulder and his ears as the gun firing that close to his head would almost definitely cause his ear drum to burst.

Taylor had taken down two of the guards by the time they reacted and decided that it was better their friend was dead than them, and they started returning fire. The guard's body jerked as the bullets entered him, causing resistance to the path Taylor was pushing him forward. The guard screamed in agony as they entered his chest and stomach, but it was the one that hit his leg that was the cause of his fall. In one swift movement, Taylor unhooked the rifles grip and now had both hands on the weapon, firing at the guards while he kept moving. A third went down as he reached cover behind a pillar.

Three down, four to go.

Taylor hadn't seen Carson, but it would be easy enough for him to hide upstairs until the intruder had been taken care of.

He crouched, assessing his situation. Bullets flew past him and hit the concrete pillar he was covering behind. He waited. Hoping one or two would come to him, then he would be able to make it a bit more of a level playing field.

The hail of bullets stopped, and silence fell. Taylor's ears were ringing from the noise, but he still listened as hard as possible for footsteps. A guard appeared to his right, his gun raised, and Taylor dropped to a crouch and fired up into him, hitting him in the chest and head. The guard hit the floor with a thud.

Another guard appeared to his right and fired. Taylor pushed off the pillar as the bullets dug in where he had once been crouched. He landed on the floor and aimed up, unleashing the AR-15 and killing another instantly. He got up and ran across to the other pillar; as he passed the fallen guard, he kicked his gun away and blind fired in the direction of the remaining guards, forcing them to take cover until it clicked to say it was empty. Once again, in the safety of cover behind the parallel pillar, Taylor swapped weapons.

Two to go.

The sound of more bullets coming at him pierced the air, and he brought his arms in and hunched to become as small as possible.

While he had been firing to cover himself for the move, he had seen their positions; they were behind identical pillars to him at the far end, but as they fired, they moved their whole bodies out. This made them a larger target and vulnerable. All he had to do was bide his time, and their mistakes would give him the opportunity he needed.

After what felt like forever, Taylor heard the guard's guns dry fire; they needed to reload.

Now or never.

He turned from behind the pillar, weapon raised, but he didn't run. He paced purposefully but smooth; he blocked out everything else, his mind calm, keeping his gun trained and reducing the amount of sway caused by his movements. One of the guards looked up, surprised by his appearance, and paused his reloading, Taylor lightly squeezed the trigger three times, and a burst of bullets shot forward, entering his chest and head in what felt like slow motion, and he fell backwards.

The other guard had been able to reload, and as he aimed and fired, Taylor was forced to take cover once again.

He waited again, but the guard seemed to have learnt and, after a moment, stopped firing. Taylor went around the outside of the pillar, in the remaining guard's blind spot and crept up forward towards his position.

The next pillar gave Taylor the view of the guard, still looking at where he had been, waiting for him to show himself. The guard had no idea that he was so close. Taylor moved around. The guard could now see him, but Taylor shot him in the leg before he could react. He fell and dropped his weapon.

Taylor came close as the guard reached out and tried to shuffle his body towards his weapon. He stood on his bullet wound; the scream echoed around the unit.

"Who else is in here?" Taylor demanded.

"Arrgh," was all he said as he winced and gripped his leg. "No one, no one, I swear."

"Where's Carson?" Taylor demanded.

"I don't know. We were told to come here and keep guard; in case anyone came looking."

"Here I am. Where is he?"

“I don’t know!” The guard cried out again as Taylor applied more pressure. “Go to hell!” He spat.
“You first,” Taylor said and shot him through the head. The echoing shot signifying the end of the conflict.

Taylor searched the rest of the unit. The ground floor was much the same, but upstairs, the offices were immaculate. There was a small boardroom with a table set up for six people, and the furniture was all wood and clean; the carpets were thick and showed little signs of wear.
This place is used for meetings, Taylor thought to himself. *This must be the Den. But why would he need to have meetings here? He has a perfectly good entire building to have them in.*
There was a lot more to Maxwell Carson than what Taylor knew about. He suspected under the table dealings and a lot more than what Geologica Industries advertises.
The only thing that mattered, though, was that Carson wasn’t here. His last effort had drawn up a blank.
He searched the drawers and paperwork he could find. There was much more here; Carson clearly used this place a lot but hid it well. Taylor searched for any signs of any other address he had, he came up with one in Spain, but that was it.

He left the unit and walked in the rain back to the car. The rain, it seemed, was to symbolise just about how he felt.

The rear driver's window glass was on the back seat, and the rock had ended up on the rear passenger footwell. The rain had covered the rear seats and spattered the interior.

He got back in the driver's seat, got out Olivia's phone to call Edgar. There was a missed call – a blocked number.

Edgar must have tried to call him during the gun fight, and he hadn't heard it.

Taylor returned his call.

"You're alive, then," Edgar said.

"For now," he replied. "But this was a dead end. He was using it for something, but he's not here now."

"I know,"

"What, how?"

"I tried to call you. He's back at his house."

Taylor started the car, slammed it into gear and floored the accelerator.

"Don't let him out of your sight!"

"I only have outside cameras man, can't tell you what he's doing inside,"

"If he leaves, tell me. Better yet, lock his fucking gate so he can't get out, and be ready to take all his electronic security down when I get there."

"I'll be ready."

Taylor hung up and continued to accelerate hard.

So, he thought to himself. You went home to die.

50

Taylor parked the BMW in the spot he had used before. Got out, noticed the broken glass from his Jaguar still on the floor, opened the boot, and dialled Edgar.

"You ready?" He asked.

"You say the word, and he won't have any electronic security or cameras available."

Taylor finished reloading, checked his weapons.

"Any idea on how many guests he has?"

"I see two outside, in the patio area, and approximately five more entered with him. But maybe more."

"Approximately?"

"Hey, I did the best I could with the angles I had; ok," Edgar explained defensively.

Taylor closed the boot and moved down the road to the house. The mud on his shoes was slipping, and he tried to slide as much as he could off before he reached the wall. He wanted as much grip available to him as possible. He put the phone to his ear.

"You ready?"

"Just give me those magic words."

"Now!" Taylor said, hanging up, dropping the phone by the wall, and scaling over.

He had scaled and thereby landed in the same spot he had the first time he had been here. There were two cars parked in the driveway. But this time, he stayed

close to the wall but moved past the kitchen window, following it to the back of the house.
A man was standing on the patio, and even though it was raining, he stood vigilant. He was wearing a grey suit. He had short, cropped hair, and he was attentive. He was no security guard. It seemed Carson had feared possible retaliation or that maybe they would send someone else to finish what Taylor had started and had surrounded himself with better security.
Taylor carefully and quietly moved around the corner. His AR-15 would alert everyone as it wasn't silenced. His Glock was, but would still make a noise, and he wanted to kill as many as possible before the bullets started flying. He softly laid his machine gun on the grass by the house wall and crept up around the man. Taylor grabbed him in a head lock and began choking him. The man resisted, but it was working. Then he heard a sound behind him, coming from inside the house. He turned, taking the guard with him in time to see another man in a similar suit emerge from the back door, realise the situation, raise, and fire his gun.
The thunder crack sound as the bullet was propelled forward destroyed any chance of this being quiet, and the bullet hit the guard in the chest. Taylor had just enough time to move away, pushing the man as a shield and dropping to the ground. He had been pressed against his back, and if the bullet had hit him, there was a chance it would have gone through the guard and into him. He withdrew his Glock from the small of his back and fired, catching the man in the chest, and he fell back onto the patio decking.

Shit! Taylor cursed himself as he got up, retrieved his AR-15 and moved towards the open back door of the house.
Just as he arrived, a man appeared; he lunged at Taylor and collided with him, sending both sprawling back outside, into the rain. Taylor had lost grip of his gun as he fell and had landed on his shoulder. A bolt of pain shot through him; whatever Olivia had given him was wearing off at the worst possible time. The guard was up again and coming for him. Taylor got to his feet, glanced around for his gun, considered drawing the Glock again, but there wasn't time. The guard was coming fast, and he didn't have the time or the space to draw and fire effectively.
The rain and the mud made Taylor's suit feel heavy, and he didn't want a drawn-out fist fight with his guy. He swung his right fist, but the guard ducked it and fired a punch to his ribs. His body felt like a hammer had hit him, and he dropped to one knee, but as he did so, he was able to block the guards left hook that was coming in. He responded by firing a jab at the guard's genitals, and that sent him reeling. Taylor stood up, he was pretty sure one more good strike to his ribs, and they would break. The guard had a knife on his belt, but he made no move to get it, and as he came back, Taylor blocked the right and the left and thought he was going to throw another right; but it was a feint, and the guard lashed out with his right leg into his knee causing Taylor to drop and expose himself. The guard moved in close, punched him across the face, and Taylor tasted blood. The guard tried to move in behind

him, to get him in a lock, but Taylor pivoted and pushed back, and they both went tumbling over the patio furniture. The guard still tried to grab as Taylor tried to get up. He had a grip on Taylor's jacket, but the mud on the back made it hard for him to get a solid hold.

Taylor let his arms slide out of the jacket as he got up, the guard now had the jacket, but with no resistance in it, he had fallen back. Taylor turned and drew his Glock from his back and fired. The guard was holding the jacket, and the bullets ripped through the crimson-coloured lining and found their mark. When his arms fell, the guard was dead, and the jacket was half on him, half on the ground and the guard's blood was mixing with the rainwater and soaking into the material. Taylor took the knife from the dead man's belt just as bullets flew past him, and he ducked behind the furniture. He heard the thud as bullets wedged themselves into the wood of the bench. He peered over and saw another guard in the doorway was firing.

He breathed deep, trying to focus, but it sent a twinge through his ribs as he inhaled. He looked for his rifle. It was on the grass where it had fallen. Not too far away. He waited for the lull in gun fire, then sprinted. His knee had been hurt in the fight, so he couldn't run as fast as he would like, but he was able to retrieve his rifle and blind fire towards the door as he took cover back in the corner he had started. His knee was throbbing from the pressure that the run had put on it, but it was nearly done; then, he would rest and allow it to heal.

Taylor took the knife out, placed his gun on the ground, crouched and waited for a guard to pursue him. A foot appeared, and he plunged the knife down, forcing it through the shoe and deep into the flesh and bone; as he pulled it out, Taylor pushed up, grabbed the guard's shirt, and dragged him around the corner and forced him against the wall. He put his hand over the guard's mouth and thrust the knife in, up under the ribcage and up into his heart. He withdrew the blade, and the man, his now lifeless eyes looking blankly at him, had died instantly, and as Taylor let go, he dropped to the floor.

He picked up his gun and moved back up to the kitchen window, where he had entered before, slid it open and climbed inside.

51

Inside the house was exactly as it had been before, except now, Taylor could hear footsteps of hard-soled shoes on wood flooring and shouting from above. The voice of Maxwell Carson carried down the stairs. He was upstairs, probably in his bedroom or office.

So that's where he would go.

He braced and moved to the door, keeping low and out of sight.

Taylor saw two men run from view to the back of the house. He was expecting Carson to make a break for it, to run, but he could still hear his voice and sounds upstairs. Once the coast was clear, he moved out and towards the stairs and climbed them cautiously, his barrel and his eyes in perfect harmony, scanning for any threats. It wasn't until he reached the landing that one appeared as two men came out of the office, clearly on their way to join the hunt. They raised their guns, but Taylor was already pulling the trigger. They were dead before they hit the floor and blood-soaked into the thick carpet beneath them. The smell of gunpowder filled the air, and the echoing of the shooting rang in his ears. Taylor moved to the office. The door had been slammed shut and locked. Taylor lined up and forced his shoulder into it, it hurt, and the door didn't open. He shot the lock, braced, and kicked it open. He entered the room, gun raised and trained on

the man who sat in the high-backed chair behind the desk.
Maxwell Carson.
"Found you," Taylor growled.
Movement came from behind him, and Taylor spun as a man entered the room. He dropped to his knee as he turned and fired on instinct, the jolt of pain reminding him of his wounded leg and almost costing him the kill shot as it was a few centimetres wide of his aim. It was still enough to kill, however, and the man fell next to the others, and as he turned back around, Taylor saw Carson out on the balcony. He fired through the glass, and the bullet found Carson's leg. He cried out and stumbled back, lost his balance, fell over the railing, and was lost from view.

Taylor left the office and made for the stairs to head down and cut off any escape attempt, but instead, he was met by three guards climbing the stairs. He was able to clear the top of the stairs and seek cover behind the wall before they started shooting, his leg was getting worse, and he was now no longer able to run. The best he could do was hobble. He returned fire, and they backed off. He had the high ground, but they had more men, and he needed to get down to deal with Carson before he escaped.
The lights in the house meant that the flash of the barrels wasn't as sharp to the eyes, but the noise was still loud, and the sound of smashing and shredding as bullets tore things apart was just as loud, and the

echoing of the big house made it seem like it was all around him.
He had to get to the back staircase.
Three men were coming up the main stairs, so that was no longer viable, and he was losing time.
Carson was escaping.

Taylor backed up, using the wall for cover. A guard came around the corner, onto the landing, he fired, and the guard fell.
Two left.
Another guard put his head around the corner and retracted it fast, Taylor fired, but the shot was wide and dug into the wall next to where the head had appeared.
He continued to back up to the stairs. He was keeping close to the wall, but the reality was he was exposed, it wouldn't take much for his position to be overrun, and that would be it. The staircase was close, though, and he was almost close enough to run and get down them; he could make it.
Out of nowhere, he was tackled to the floor. His gun was sent skidding away from him, and there was a man over him. The guard punched down, and he had to block; he was weak and too slow; however, while he could cushion part of the blow, there was still enough to send his head rocking back and hitting the floor.
Taylor's vision of the hallway was sent spinning, and his brain felt like it had been smashed against his skull.
He struggled to regain focus. He kept his arms up, blocking as best he could, waiting for his head to recalibrate and allow him to retaliate. The guard kept

punching. He knew he had the intruder on the ropes, and sooner or later, he would land the finishing blow. Taylor was still dazed but became cognitive enough to react. He grabbed the guard's arm as he punched again, pulled his body close and sunk his teeth as hard as he could into his ear. The guard cried out in pain and arched back. Taylor punched him in the throat and rolled him off. The guard with the gun on the stairs had halted his attack, it wasn't a clear shot when the two men were grappling on the floor, but now that his colleague had been rolled off, he had a clear shot. Taylor rolled behind the guard and lifted him up enough to use him as a shield. The bullets that were meant for him hit the guard, and he stopped moving. Taylor reached and grabbed his gun, still using the downed guard as a shield; he looked over and fired, shooting the advancing guard in the chest and removing him as a threat.

Gun fire stopped. The guard that had come at him from behind must have been the other guard on the main stairs that had doubled back and come at him from behind.

Why didn't he just shoot him, though? Taylor thought himself lucky as he took a moment in the quiet to get himself right, then he got up and moved to the back staircase and started making his way down, heavy-footed, using the rail to support his body weight. Everywhere smelled of gun powder and blood, there was a ringing in his ear, and he was limping, but he was still going. Determined, mind focused on his task.

At the bottom of the stairs, he was greeted by a lone guard hiding behind some furniture, Taylor should have spotted him waiting, but he didn't. The shot rang out, and Taylor's leg was taken out from under him. He cried out with pain as the bullet passed through, and he dropped to the floor. Agony screamed from the wound to his brain; it felt like fire and lightning, just like it had before.
Getting shot never got less painful.
His AR-15 had been dropped and was out of reach, but he still had his Glock. The guard hadn't seen it, and sure of his victory, he came out from cover to get up close and personal to kill him. Taylor was on his back, so he rolled, drawing his weapon as he moved and fired twice once he was lying on his stomach. The guard looked surprised and made to raise his own weapon, but the two bullets entered his chest.
The gun never finished raising. The surprised look on his face was the man's last.

It took a minute for Taylor to get up. When he had rolled, he had put pressure on his wound, and it was making him feel lightheaded and sick. He quickly assessed the fresh gunshot wound to his leg and deduced that it wasn't too bad; it was more of a through and through graze. Nothing vital was hit, and he would be able to walk on it.
He slowly got up and tried to keep his gun ready for whoever came next. His body was almost spent, whatever Olivia had given him had worn off, and he was struggling to force his body to keep vigilant for the

next threat. But nobody came. No new threat revealed itself.

Silence lay upon the house. The only thing he could hear was the groans of a man outside. Taylor walked through the house and out the back door. The bodies of the guards he had fought earlier were lying peacefully on the ground where they had fallen.

Taylor put another bullet in each one to make sure as he walked past.

On the grass, down the long garden, a man pulled himself along the ground. It looked like he was army crawling, except his right leg was dragging behind him. There was a faint trail of blood in the wet grass, reminiscent of a snail trail that followed behind him. Maxwell Carson was trying to crawl his way to the woods.

52

The sound of the gun shots behind him had caused him to turn around, and Carson saw the man standing in the patio area, looking down the long garden at him. Panic set in; he knew he had to escape. He was in more pain than he had ever been in. His leg was in agony, and he winced every time it was dragged over the grass, the smallest distance sent more pain through it, but he knew he would have to just keep going if he wanted to get away. If he wanted to survive.
He would get away, he would re-group, and he would find this son-of-a-bitch, and he would make him pay; he was determined of that.
Carson glanced back again and saw the man coming towards him. More fear, more panic flooded through his body. He was out of protection, and he couldn't outrun him.

A realisation settled in his mind, and while instinct told him to keep moving, keep going, he knew it was in vain.
He knew he was beaten.
He was crawling away, but he had nowhere to go, nowhere that he could get to that would be safe before the man in the black suit would get to him.
Carson risked another glance back.

The man was coming for him.

53

Logan Taylor watched Carson for a moment, slowly inching away, he had briefly looked back when he had fired the shots into his men, but now he was back to crawling away.

The air was damp, and he smelt wet clothes – probably his – the rain had died off a bit now, but it had rained most of the night. The mud and moisture were causing the back of his trousers to cling to his legs, and without the adrenaline of fighting, he realised how it restricted his movements.

He had been looking forward to this moment, though.

This was what the whole night had been about.

This was for the woman Carson had tortured and burned.

This was for destroying his car and trying to have him killed.

This was for Olivia.

This was for all the others that had been and gone under this man's self-issued death warrants.

It ended tonight.

He started walking down the grass towards him.

Taylor walked towards Carson, the grass masking the sounds of his footsteps. The bullet wound in his leg caused him to limp even more, and each step now sent a new wave of pain through his body. He grimaced against it but limped on, his eyes locked on his target.

He reached him, and Carson knew it was over, he must have, but his survival instinct was still telling him to flee, to try and get distance, to run.
Taylor shot him through the back of the knee of his other leg, and Carson screamed a cry of anguish into the night.
He stopped moving, he rolled over, and now they were face to face.
"Who the fuck do you think you are?" Carson said, pure hatred in his voice; he spat the words like venom as he gripped his knee, trying to relinquish the pain.
Taylor said nothing and just looked down at him.
"You have no idea what you are involved in. You're just a puppet! You are here to advance someone else's game; you're a pawn! You're nothing! You were used so they could take my company! That's why you're here, you fucking piece of shit!"
Taylor stayed quiet for a moment. He looked down at the man lying on the ground in front of him.
"Actually, Mr Carson," he said finally, "I'm here because of you. Everything that has happened tonight has stemmed from the moment you made the call after I left your bedroom. Tonight, I am the Grim Reaper, and I have come for you."
"Fuck you!" Carson retaliated, "I can pay you, pay you to go away, or I can lead you to the people that set you on me, you could go after them, you could actually take down those fuckers." There was a note of pleading in his voice. "It was just business." Carson reasoned.
Taylor considered telling him that it wasn't his business to know what the bigger picture was; he was

simply the middleman, that was what he was. He was a means to someone's end. That was what The Company did; he didn't care who had put out the contract or why. It wasn't for him to know.
He could have explained that all this had come from Carson's actions towards him, the woman he had tortured, and Olivia.
He thought about explaining all of this, but instead, he looked down at Maxwell Carson, his face white as a ghost, the sweat dripping from his body, the scared look in his eye that he tried to mask with his defiance and anger, the two gunshot wounds that kept him from moving and said, "it was business, until you made it personal."
Then Taylor looked Carson in the eye as he pulled the trigger twice more, shooting him in the heart.

Maxwell Carson died instantly.

Taylor then put a bullet in his head because he deserved it.

Then Logan Taylor turned and limped back through the house, past all the silent, motionless bodies of the men Carson had surrounded himself with in a last-ditch effort to stop the inevitable. Edgar opened the gate for him as he walked down the drive, the gravel catching in his foot like a plough as he dragged his leg. He collected the phone by the wall, got back to the BMW and drove away.

54

One week later

After the Carson incident, Taylor had driven home and reported back to the room on the third floor of the tattoo studio. After his initial debrief explaining what had happened regarding the contract, he then had a meeting with the Administrator.
Once everything had been explained and filed away, The Company had sent out a team to clean up and work containment of the Carson house and the other affected properties and locations.
It would be dealt with efficiently and monitored closely in case anything came to light with authorities that would implicate Taylor or The Company in any of his actions over the past few days. Taylor straightened it all up and made sure Edgar received no repercussions of what he did to help him.
He had then sort out medical attention. The Company had told him too, but in his heart, he knew he was doing it because of Olivia.
He had gotten stitched and patched up, and he was now slowly on the mend. He had been taken off the active list again until further notice and been told to relax and recover.
When he had returned home, he had heard on the TV about a police officer who had committed suicide in his home during an internal investigation into the death of

a man in his custody. It was of no interest to him, so he just turned the TV off again.

Taylor had done as requested for the next few days; he kept his head down, relaxed in the apartment, and allowed his body to start its recovery. Even if he returned to the studio, he knew they would not allow him to return to active status, so he allowed himself his downtime.
However, he had followed Edgar up on the laptop from the woman's car to see if he knew who she was. Edgar had told him that all the laptop contained was things they already knew; it was most likely a burner. They had drawn a blank on her identification too.
He booked a hotel and decided that he wanted to get away for a while. So, he packed a small case, put it in the boot of the Alfa Romeo and took a short vacation.

He had visited The Star Palace Café every day since he had arrived, at various times, but had had no luck. On the third night, however, he got what he came for.
It was around eleven pm, and the night was dark, a few stars shone in the sky, but most were hidden from view by the clouds that drifted along on the breeze. It was a nice night, warm and dry. Justine was out the back again, Alex Croft was with her, once again with her pinned up against the skip waste container. Taylor had considered visiting him at home, but he wanted to do it here, where Croft felt he had power. Taylor wanted to take it away from him.

He walked around the back of the café and up to the scene.
“Excuse me,” Taylor said, “can I get something to eat?”
Justine looked over at him, the same look she had before.
Croft turned, it took him a moment, but once he recognised Taylor, his body changed, he stood up tall, puffed his chest out as he said, “you’re brave, coming back here, thought you’d learnt your lesson, do you remember what I told you that I would do if I saw you again.”
“I do, yes.” Nodded Taylor
“An’ now you’re gonna get it.” Croft walked towards Taylor and was very sure of himself. He was a man who was used to getting his way, mainly through fear. But Taylor wasn’t afraid of him. He also didn’t have anywhere else he needed to be, so he had all the time in the world.
Croft, it seemed, had been expecting him to step back or cower and try to disarm the situation.
This time Taylor didn’t.
Taylor could see Justine over Croft’s shoulder. She had her shoulders hunched and her hands over her mouth. She knew what he was capable of, but she seemed too scared to try and stop him this time. She also had a nasty cut on her lip.
Croft approached; he seemed hell-bent on carrying out his threat, asserting his dominance, so Taylor let him. Croft threw his first punch, a right hook, his dominant hand. Taylor caught it at the wrist and flipped Croft to

the ground in one smooth motion. Croft, now on his front with his right arm stretched out behind him, cried out in pain as Taylor put tension through it.
"Now," Taylor said, quiet and calm, his voice just above a whisper, "I remember you were going to break my fingers, weren't you?"
Croft just lay there, his teeth gritted as he tried to endure the pain.
"So, let's do that," Taylor said.
He pulled Croft's index finger back, and the bone snapped, breaking his finger. Croft cried out in agony, and then he just started crying and sobbing at the pain.
"Are you ever going to contact Justine again?" Taylor asked.
"No, no man, no," Croft sobbed.
"Are you ever going to speak to her again?"
"No, never. I swear."
"Look at her again?"
"No, please, please."
"If I hear so much as you have looked at her the wrong way, or any of your clown friends try anything towards her, I'll come back for you. I mean, I want you to cross the street when you see her walking and put your head down in fear in case you accidentally make eye contact. That understood?" Taylor put more pressure on his arm, and he yelled out in pain.
"Ok, ok, ok. I won't. They won't, I promise," Croft spluttered through the tears streaming down his face.
"I'm not fucking around," Taylor said, "I know everything about you, Alexander Graham Croft. I know where you live, I know who your friends are, I

know where you like to go, I know what car you drive. I am not the man you try and double-cross. Understand?"
"Yes, yes, mate, I understand, I promise, please let go of my arm; it hurts so bad." Croft whimpered.
Taylor let go and looked up at Justine. He took a card out of his pocket and handed it to her.
"He looks at you again," Taylor said, "you call me."
Justine just looked at him and nodded, then she ran past them both and back into the café, pulling the door closed behind her.
Taylor walked back to where Croft was lying on the floor, cradling his arm and holding his hand close to his chest. Taylor stood over him.
"Why did you beat her?" Taylor asked.
"I'm sorry, I shouldn't have. I'm sorry,"
"No, you're right. You shouldn't have. I asked why."
"I don't know; she would do what she was told. I'm sorry, mate."
Taylor made a finger gun shape with his hand and pointed it at Croft, just like Croft had done to him the time before when they were both out here, in the night air, behind the café, only this time, after doing it, Taylor drew his weapon and pointed it straight at Croft's face. Alex Croft wept, put his hands up to try and protect his face, and urinated himself with fear.
"I'm not your mate," Taylor said, "don't make me come back here."
"Ok, ok, ok man, ok, ok, I promise." Croft pleaded, lowering his hands. He had tears running down his face.

“Never lay your hands on a woman like that again,” he said, “and here’s a reminder.” Taylor kicked him hard in the face with the bottom of his foot, the heel crashing into his nose, breaking it, and cutting his lip. Croft curled up into a heap on the floor, weeping and sobbing.
Taylor turned and walked away into the night.
It wouldn’t set right the things he had done, the people he had gotten killed, but it helped ease his conscience a little.

He returned home the following day, and after he settled in, he went to the studio. He didn’t go to work, and he didn’t try to get put back on the active list. He decided he would make the most of his time.
He sat in Sam’s chair, and he got a tattoo of a black cartoon bomb on his right lower arm, as he promised himself he would.

As the needle put the ink into his skin, Taylor reflected on the last couple of weeks as a whole, from Brandon Houton and the bomb explosion to everything with The White Lion to the Carson incident and how he had moments when he was sure he was going to die.

But now he was sitting here, in the studio, getting a tattoo, and he couldn’t help wondering what would come in his next assignment.

55

The Chairman had called a meeting of the Committee, and once again, everybody had attended; it would have been foolish not to.

He sat in the same chair as he had when all this had started, looking down at the same table and the same faces, only now there were two empty chairs.

One was his doing, but one wasn't.

"Thank you all for coming," he welcomed. "I am pleased to announce that we are now in control of Geologica Industries." He paused and looked down the table; people were nodding their approval.

"This continues us forward to our plans," The Chairman continued, "but it was not without cost." He looked at the empty seat where the woman had sat. She had never returned from England.

"Gemini succeeded in her mission, Carson is dead, and we have what we need, but she lost her life in the process. This will not stand. She will be avenged. I will not allow people thinking they can take out our people; it will be allowed."

More head nodding.

"Aries, you will find who did this to her, and you will deal with it. Do I make myself clear?"

A man down the table, a big man in a dark grey suit, nodded once.

"Good, the rest of us will continue with our work and move forward onto the next phase. There is still much work to be done. That is all."
The Chairman then stood up and walked out.

As the men and women left the table one by one, returning to their 'normal' jobs, keeping this cabal that The Committee had created in power, the man known as Aries remained seated, so still, he could have been mistaken for a statue.
He was preparing himself. He would take his time; he would find the best time and place to do what needed to be done. He would not fail, and he would not suffer the same fate as Gemini.

When he was ready, Aries got up and set about his task of hunting down the man who had killed the woman who had travelled to England, the woman known to him only as Gemini.

THE END.

The new assignment for The Company;
The Phoenix Initiative
Is now available

About The Author

Mark Reddan was born in Northamptonshire. While working many jobs, he had a passion for artwork and writing short scripts and screenplays, but when he discovered his love of Tattooing, he paused writing to pursue the life of an artist.

Art, and inspiration come in many forms, and during the Covid-19 lockdown of 2021, he woke up one morning with the idea for Agent Red, and The Company fully formed in his mind and decided to write the story down. It took just over two weeks for the first draft of his first novel – 'Agent Red' to be completed. There were no ambitions to make it available to the public – it was just for him and him alone, but when he shared it with his wife, she soon had a social media presence and a website in development to help him reach an audience.

He currently lives in the Southwest of England with his wife Sarah, and writes around working as a tattoo artist.

www.markreddan.co.uk

Printed in Great Britain
by Amazon

70027138R00182